Lynching at Prospect Falls

Jack Matthews

A Black Horse Western

ROBERT HALE · LONDON

© Jack Matthews 2014
First published in Great Britain 2014

ISBN 978-0-7198-1411-2

Robert Hale Limited
Clerkenwell House
Clerkenwell Green
London EC1R 0HT

www.halebooks.com

Typeset by
Derek Doyle & Associates, Shaw Heath
Printed and bound in Great Britain by
CPI Antony Rowe, Chippenham and Eastbourne

1

'Don't touch that rifle,' Jez Moxley ordered, his heavily accentuated voice mean and purposeful. At four inches over six feet, Moxley was a big man, broad and powerfully muscled. He stood motionless, blocking the sun, his wide features covered in shadow.

The young man's hand moved an inch or two more.

'Let it lay, I said.' The wooden stock of the Winchester crashed down on the young man's head. Moxley turned. 'He's one of 'em, boss. Certain of it.'

The morning air was crisp and still as the first rays of daylight broke over the eastern hills. Henry John Copeland wiped his nose on the back of one expensive leather glove, then spoke.

'Tie him up. Take his guns,' he said, brushing a stray leaf from the lapel of his corduroy coat.

Two of the eight cowboys with him jumped down from their horses to obey their boss's command.

Henry Copeland stepped down from his horse. He pointed at the pot set on a stone at the edge of the still glowing fire.

'Give me some of that coffee.'

A cowboy washed out a tin cup using water from the young man's canteen, and poured out a cupful of steaming liquid. He handed it to his boss.

'Good coffee,' Copeland commented, licking his thin lips. He wiped a few drops off his drooping moustache.

The golden sun was high in the sky when the young man next opened his eyes. He tried to focus on the group of men standing around him; each was a blurred grey shadow. Half a canteen of water was emptied over the young man's bare head. He flinched, and made to wipe water from his eyes; that was when he realized his hands were tied behind him. He was still having trouble focusing.

'Wh . . . who are you? Wh . . . what's this all about? I haven't done anything,' the young man stammered out. His pleading words raised one or two chuckles. Sombre, featureless faces swam into view as his vision cleared a little.

'Get him on his horse,' Copeland ordered, taking a long thin cigar out of an expensively tooled leather case. He bit off the end and spat it out. 'Match,' he said loudly. A heavy-set cowboy with a scar on his right cheek obliged. 'Thanks, Tex,' said Copeland, blowing out a smoke ring. 'Name?'

'I haven't done anything, mister,' the young man protested as rough hands dragged him to his feet. He struggled in vain against the ropes that threatened to squeeze the life out of him.

Henry Copeland blew out more smoke. 'I said what's your name, boy?'

Their victim was too startled to say much. 'Wh . . . What?'

Moxley took a step forward and slapped the youth hard across the mouth. 'Answer Mr Copeland.'

The young man's tongue flicked out the corner of his mouth, tasting the salty blood on his lips. He hesitated to answer until he saw the big man's arm sweep upwards to strike him again.

'Crane. J . . . Joseph Crane,' he stammered out. His voice was soft, light in tone; almost pubescent.

Copeland eyed the young man with little or no emotion. 'Where you from?'

'Arkansas.'

'How old are you?'

'Nineteen. Nearly twenty.'

Henry Copeland nodded to the big man, recalling Moxley's words: *Sure we can keep runnin' 'em off, boss, but sooner or later we need to take a stand. Take a harder line. Set an example. Show these vagrants that takin' Bar C beef carries a heavy penalty.* He knew Moxley was right.

The ropes binding Joseph Crane's feet were cut. Two men grabbed a leg each, two others grabbed the young man under his arms. For more than ten minutes he fought against the vicelike grips that carried him to where another man held his horse. Eventually they got him on to the sorrel's bare back.

Jez Moxley threw a rope over the sturdiest limb of the tall tree under which the young man had made his camp the previous night. The noose at the rope's end swung gently from side to side. Two cowboys rode their horses either side of the young man's, holding him and his horse tight.

'Anything you want to say?' Henry Copeland asked.

The young man looked up and saw the noose. A sudden realization of what was about to happen hit home like an arrow in his chest. A breeze got up, ruffling his straw-coloured hair. One of the cowboys tried to loop the noose over the young man's head, but the youth jerked his head away, screaming the word '*No*' over and over.

'Hold his head still,' shouted Moxley.

Eventually the noose was in place. Tears of disbelief streamed down the young man's cheeks.

'I haven't done anything,' he cried, struggling against his bonds. 'Don't do this. Please. Please. Cut me loose,' his terrified voice screamed out.

Henry Copeland ground the stub of his cigar on the hard earth with his boot heel, nodding to the big man.

'No!' The young man screamed, as Moxley slapped the sorrel's rump. 'No!' The young man screamed yet again as the horse surged forward.

The noose tightened, choking off the young man's screams. The branch cracked with a sound like a thunder-clap, but held. The young man's legs twitched and jerked in a macabre dance. The grim-faced cowboys watched the body writhe on the taut line until the legs were still; then, their grisly work done, they looked to their boss for instructions.

'Gather up his stuff, and his horse, then get back to the ranch,' said Copeland.

Tex Grimes had a hold of the kid's horse and saddle, Bob Andrews had gathered up his belongings.

'Want me to cut him down, boss?' asked Moxley.

'No. Just pin this on his chest.' The rancher held out a

piece of paper on which he had written the word RUSTLER; underneath he had added the name JOSEPH CRANE. 'Leave him there as a warning to anyone who thinks they can steal my beef.'

Two of the eight cowhands protested at the lynching, but were cowed by the big man.

'You don't like it,' Moxley told them menacingly, 'you can make tracks now.'

'What about our wages?' one demanded.

'Anybody leaves forfeits their pay,' yelled Henry Copeland. 'He got what he deserved. Now get back to the ranch, pronto.'

'How do we know he was one of the rustlers?'

'Jez here caught him red-handed.' Copeland fitted his left foot into the patterned silver stirrup and swung a leg over his horse's back. 'He's been eating steak. Look at the pan.'

The disbelieving cowboy ambled sheepishly over to the dying embers. He drew a long-bladed knife from a scabbard on his belt and flipped what remained of the young man's breakfast.

'Bacon!' he called out. 'It's bacon. Bacon and beans!'

The big man grabbed the cowboy's arm. 'That's because he'd already eaten the steak,' yelled Jez Moxley. 'Now let it go!'

The cowboy snatched his arm free. 'But. . . .' his protest was stilled by Moxley's huge fist.

The cowboy was dumped unceremoniously on his backside, and made the mistake of reaching for his six-gun. The big man was faster. He drew his Colt and shot the cowboy between the eyes. Moxley swivelled, levelling the

Colt. 'Anybody else?'

The other cowboys made sure they kept their hands well clear of their side-irons. Their faces looked gaunt, their expressions were strained, most of them not quite believing the sequence of events they had witnessed on that chilly September morning, despite having seen such scenes many times before.

Moxley kicked out the fire, then mounted his horse.

'Drape him,' he gestured towards the dead cowhand, 'over his horse. Let's get back to the ranch.'

The sombre procession filed out of the clearing. The last two cowboys to leave took anything they could. One pulled off the young man's boots, the other cleaned out his pockets, took his gun belt, and belt. He had intended to take the fairly new-looking denims until he saw the stains where the young man had fouled himself.

The lifeless body, clad only in a grey-flannel shirt and soiled denims, swung gently on the breeze for a long time after the lynching party had left. Just before sundown, the branch splintered a second time with a loud crack. The body jerked a couple of feet nearer the earth, but held.

'You gonna eat that piece of steak?'

Marshal Matt Walker glared at the questioner. 'You just keep your eyes off it, if you know what's good for you,' he said, and laughed.

Ed Massey clapped his friend on the shoulder,

'OK, you keep it. You look like you need it more than me.'

Mrs Regan heard the laughter and came into the dining room.

10

'You boys just about finished?' She was intent upon clearing away the dishes. Matt pushed back his chair with the backs of his legs.

'Finished,' he said, popping the last piece of meat into his mouth. He stretched his tall, lean frame. 'Mrs Regan, that was delicious. It's a shame you're already married.' He gave her a peck on the cheek.

'You're a cheeky young varmint for a marshal,' she scolded, secretly pleased to have been kissed. Ed grinned at her. 'And you, Ed Massey, you're just as bad as your boss.'

'What did I do?' Ed said innocently.

'Get out of here,' she joked. 'Get back to work.'

Matt looked up at the big clock on the wall. 'She's right, Ed,' he said, hitching up his denims, then strapping on his gunbelt. 'Time for our evening rounds.'

Ed picked up his hat and gunbelt and followed Matt to the door.

' 'Night, Mrs Regan,' they chorused, closing the door behind them.

The two-storey jailhouse and town marshal's office was half a block from Mrs Regan's café. The light from a solitary lantern showed dimly through the window blinds. Matt rapped four times on the door.

'OK, Marshal, it's open,' called out Deputy Dan Meacham.

Matt lifted the latch and entered, Ed at his shoulder. Behind the big oak desk Dan stretched and yawned, then sauntered lazily over to the stove and poured himself a cup of coffee.

'Enjoy your supper?' he enquired.

11

'Yep,' Ed replied, grabbing a cup from the shelf. He held it out so that Dan could fill it. The coffee wasn't hot. Ed drained the cup and set it down. He selected a Winchester from the gun rack, checked it was loaded and tossed it to Matt, then grabbed another for himself. Both men tucked a handful of extra shells into their pockets.

'Prisoners OK?' Matt asked.

Dan cocked an ear. 'Sound asleep. Can't you hear them?' He opened a door at the rear of the room. The snores drifted downstairs to the marshal's office from the first-floor cells.

Ed opened the door to the street for Matt. 'See you in an hour,' he said.

Dan raised a hand and returned to his seat behind the desk. One booted foot resting on the desk, he built a smoke, blew out a smoke ring, then settled down to wait for Matt and Ed to get back, so he could get off home. Tonight it was Ed's turn for the night shift. Dan drew in a mouthful of smoke and closed his eyes; he could almost taste that first glass of cool beer he would order in O'Leary's bar. He smacked his lips and settled down.

The sound of the two lawmen's boots echoed through the dark street. The few citizens they passed bade them a goodnight and wished them well. A grey dog ran across the rutted Main Street, parts of which were still muddy after a recent cloudburst. The dog sniffed at everything it passed, the colour of its fur changing from grey to gold in the light of a streetlamp. Both saloons were quiet, sparsely populated by one or two well-known late-night drinkers and a couple of harmless-looking drifters. In the

Alhambra saloon a friendly card game was under way and, judging from the pile of chips in front of him, Doc Wainwright appeared to be winning. His happy expression contrasted strongly with the griping look on the mayor's face opposite.

Both greeted the lawmen warmly, as did the other two hopeful gamblers: storekeeper Milt Delaney and Vern Elliot, the barber-cum-undertaker.

The round of the town proved to be uneventful. All was quiet and peaceful, as it had been for the best part of a year since Matt Walker had been appointed town marshal of Sweetwater Springs. He and his two deputies had run out the unwanted elements that had arrived during the brief silver boom.

On returning to the jail Ed put away the Winchesters and locked the gun rack. Dan said goodnight, leaving the two lawmen alone.

'Want a cup of coffee before you get off home?' Ed asked, pleased to find that Dan had brewed a fresh pot.

'Sure. I'll take one with you.'

Ed poured out two cups. He looked at the marshal, believing there was something troubling him.

'When you expectin' your nephew to arrive?' he asked. 'Didn't his wire say he was planning to get here over a week ago?'

'Yep. Should have arrived before now. He was taking the new train line to Odessa in Texas, bringing his horse with him. Then from there he was planning to ride the rest of the way. Wants to see more of the Wild West he's read about, apparently.' Matt frowned. 'Guess he's taking his own sweet time. Crazy kid.'

'Probably met some nice young lady on the way and decided to sow some wild oats.'

'Maybe,' said Matt. He didn't show it, but Joey's non-arrival troubled him.

2

A week later when there was still no sign of the kid, Matt's mild concern grew into something graver. He decided to telegraph his sister to ask if Joey had been delayed.

Her reply came next day; she was obviously worried. Her wire said that Joey had left on time and that she hadn't heard from him for over a week. The wire said she had sent Matt a letter outlining Joey's proposed route, asking him to go look for him, and that she had telegraphed Joey's uncle, her dead husband's elder brother, asking him to help. Bob Crane was an army scout attached to General Swift's Third Cavalry at Fort James in southern Colorado.

Her letter arrived a few days later, confirming all she had said in her wire, and enclosing a tintype picture of Joey taken only a few months earlier, along with one of her and her daughter, Hannah.

Matt read and reread his sister's letter with more than a little concern. In it she mentioned that Bob had telegraphed to say he was on his way to Sweetwater Springs.

Matt was not convinced of the merits of going out on what might prove to be a wild-goose chase, but it seemed the die was cast. Now he felt unable to refuse his sister's request. He recalled what he knew about the scout.

In his time Bob Crane had been a lawman, then a cavalry officer during the War between the States; now he was chief of scouts for General Swift. Matt had only met Bob three times; the first occasion had been at his sister's wedding to Bob's younger brother. Matt remembered he hadn't liked him much – a big bluff Westerner of very few words but with a fearsome reputation. *Arrogant*: that was the word Matt would have chosen to best describe Bob Crane. It had been the same on the second occasion, at baby Joey's baptism. Nothing had changed to alter Matt's view of the man. However, on their third meeting Matt revised his opinion totally. At the funeral of his sister's husband Bob had been attentive, considerate, kind: all qualities Matt had never seen before.

Next day Matt received a telegram from Bob, saying he would arrive in Sweetwater Springs by the fourteenth of the month. Matt showed Ed all the correspondence.

'That's the day after tomorrow,' said the deputy.

Ed looked with interest at the map of the territory that Matt spread out of the desk, and watched the marshal mark Joey's route with a red pencil. Matt recognized the risks of making assumptions that failed to allow for rivers in flood and for the contours of the land that Joey would have to pass through. He studied the areas he knew would be the most difficult to cross, ringing them in red. He straightened up, the small of his back aching a little.

'I'd say this is the most likely way Joey will come.' He had made a note of the towns and settlements between Sweetwater Springs and Odessa. 'I'll ride the route in reverse,' he told Ed. 'Hopefully I'll find him not far away from here.'

A little before noon Bob Crane rode into Sweetwater Springs on a fine looking dun, leading a sturdy packhorse. He hitched his horses outside the jail and stepped inside the office. Ed looked up from the desk at the buckskin-clad giant of a man standing before him.

'Name's Bob Crane. I'm looking for Marshal Walker.'

Ed walked out from behind the desk, and stuck out a hand. 'Ed Meacham, one of Matt's deputies. Glad to meet you.' He smiled. 'I'll get Matt.' He stepped out on to the stoop and stopped a passing boy. 'Go over to Mrs Regan's, tell the marshal Bob Crane is here.'

The boy scooted off down the street, and in less than ten minutes Matt Walker entered his office.

'Howdy, Bob.' He held out a hand. The two men shook hands warmly.

'Long time no see,' said Bob. After hearing Matt's plan, he asked. 'Do you want to start out now or wait till tomorrow?'

'Now, if it's OK with you. There's a lot of daylight left.'

Bob smiled. 'Now it is, then.'

'Let me get my stuff together. Ed, will you get my horse and packhorse from the livery?'

'Sure.' Ed left in a hurry.

'Everything's ready,' said Matt, selecting a Winchester from the rack. 'Just need to load the rest of my gear on to my horses. You toting everything you need?'

'Yes. I'm all set.'

Ed came in, breathing heavily, beads of sweat on his hatless forehead; he had obviously been running. 'Horses are out front, all saddled and packed.'

Matt slipped on a khaki coat, strapped on a pair of spurs, and adjusted his gunbelt. He handed Ed the Winchester and a couple of boxes of shells, grabbed a long decorated rifle scabbard from the rack, and followed Ed out to the horses.

'See you still got that old long-range Sharps .50-90,' the scout observed.

'Wouldn't be without it,' answered Matt. 'This old piece has got me out of many a potentially tight situation.'

Ed busied himself packing the shells, and sliding the Winchester into the saddle boot. Matt slid the long scabbard containing the Sharps under the cinch on the other side of his horse.

The Sweetwater Springs town council had been divided on the subject of Matt's request to take some time off work for personal reasons. Finally, after long consideration, the mayor had cast his deciding vote in Matt's favour. Matt was also pleased that the council had accepted his recommendation that Ed be promoted acting town marshal in his absence.

'Look, Pa.' Jebadiah Ekstold pointed. 'A body.'

Josiah Ekstold reined in his old nag alongside his son.

18

'Where?' he demanded, squinting into the heat haze with his one good eye – his fading eyesight caused everything to be covered in a milky cloud.

Their mounts moved a few steps forward. 'There, Pa. Hangin' offa that tree.'

'Yeah. I see it now, boy.'

The head hung limply down, chin on his chest, face burned dark by the unrelenting sun, hands much lighter in colour, bare feet pointing at the ground.

A couple of sour-faced vultures flapped away as Jebadiah spurred his mule to where the body swung slowly.

'Want me t'cut 'im down, Pa?'

'Sure,' said Josiah, swinging down from his horse's back.

The rigid corpse hit the dry earth with a dull thud, sending up a thin cloud of chalky dust. The smell was none too good. The old man prodded the body with a well-worn boot.

'Turn 'im over. Let's get a proper look at 'im.'

Jebadiah grabbed an arm and turned the body over. Sightless eye sockets stared up at them, the eyeballs having been pecked out by birds. Some toes and fingers were missing. A gaping wound encrusted with dried blood gaped from the back of the corpse's head.

Hitching up the rope belt that held up his patched trousers Jebadiah went down on one knee to examine the face closely.

'Aw, Pa, what a mess. Not even his ma would recognize 'im.'

The old man bent forward, wrinkling his bulbous nose.

'What's this?' He snatched up the soiled piece of paper

pinned to the corpse's tattered shirt and examined it, turning it over a few times in his grubby hands. Neither he nor his son could read, so he screwed the paper into a ball and shoved it into a pocket. He set about making a search of the body, tut-tutting disappointedly at finding nothing at all in the shirt or denim pockets. He pulled at the shredded material covering the upper part of the body.

'Shirt and pants ain't no good. Critters have pulled too many holes in 'em.' He stood up and picked at his teeth with a sliver of wood he'd found.

'What shall we do with 'im, Pa?'

Josiah thought for a moment. 'Put 'im on the back of yer mule.'

'What fer?'

'Do as I tell ya, boy.'

'But Pa. . . ?'

'Prospect Falls is the nearest town. We'll take 'im there, see if we can find a buyer.'

His son looked incredulously at his father. 'Heck, Pa,' he guffawed, 'who'd want to buy a dead body?'

'He's got a good set of teeth. I'll find me somebody to make me up a new set of false teeth out of 'em. These wooden things are killin' me.'

'You can't do that, Pa, it ain't right.'

'He ain't got no more use for 'em.'

'Who makes false teeth, Pa?'

'Dentists!' his father snapped. 'Dentists buy teeth. Surgeons buy bodies. Stupid.' Josiah looked around. 'Anyhow, where's your stupid brother?'

'Dunno, Pa. Ain't seen 'im since he stopped off to relieve himself near that big cactus back a ways. Hope he don't spike his pecker.' He chuckled.

'Quiet,' the old man shouted. He settled his aching body down in the shade of the hanging tree and pulled his battered fedora low over his face. 'I need some shut-eye.'

Jebadiah struggled manfully, but eventually got the body on to the mule's back, hogtying the hands and feet under the animal's belly.

'Ready, Pa,' he called out. He crossed to where his father lay. 'Here's what was round his neck. I got the rest of the rope coiled on my mule.' Pleased with himself, he held out a grubby hand to pull the old man to his feet.

The old man unleashed a string of obscenities at his creaking bones, then said, 'Thanks, son. Well done.' Both heads turned to face the noise of an animal behind them.

'It's OK, Pa, it's only Gideon,' said Jebadiah.

'Where you bin?' Josiah shouted, seeing who it was. He swung a slap at Jebadiah for no reason, but the lad twisted away. Josiah ambled over as his younger son, a boy of sixteen or seventeen, reined in his mule and stepped down.

'I axed you where you bin?' Josiah repeated.

Ignoring his father's question, the lad pointed. 'What's that?' he asked.

Josiah slapped him on the back of his head. 'I axed you where you bin?'

'Nowhere, Pa. Honest.' Gideon rubbed his head, eyeing his father sheepishly.

At one hour past nightfall the three vagrants reached Prospect Falls.

The clothes of all three were well worn and scruffy.

21

Their hands and faces were filthy, each of them had many teeth missing. Gideon had a permanent grin on his simple face, making him look more stupid than he was.

'If nobody's around we'll bed down at the livery stable,' Josiah said. But as the procession of three neared the stable a man stepped out from the shadows, holding a lantern at head height. In the crook of his other arm he cradled an eight-gauge shotgun.

'If you want the livery it's closed up for the night,' he said.

'Oh. Name's Josiah Ekstold. These are my two boys,' Josiah gestured. 'Jebadiah and Gideon.'

The man with the lantern nodded. 'And who might that be?' he asked, motioning toward the body.

'Dead. Don't know his name,' replied Josiah. 'Found it.'

'Where?'

'What?' queried the old man.

Jebadiah butted in. 'He said . . . Oh never mind. I'll tell it. Pa's a bit deaf. We found 'im east of here. Fifteen, twenty miles outside town. Hangin' from a tree. Lynched! Bin there a long time, I'd say, judging by the smell he's givin' off.' He screwed up his face. 'Critters have pecked it up a bit.'

The man took a step forward. 'Hold this.' He thrust the lantern at Jebadiah and grabbed a hunk of hair. His nose wrinkled when he lifted up the limp head. 'Shine that light closer,' he ordered, holding his nose as he examined what remained of the features. 'Don't recognize him. Young fella though, I'd say. Like you say, he stinks a bit.'

'What?'

'I said, he stinks a bit.'

'Huh?' queried Josiah, wondering if he had heard right. 'Hadn't noticed,' he said.

The man wanted to say: *no wonder you can't smell it – you stink almost as bad.* He wanted to, but thought better of it.

Josiah fished the crumpled-up piece of paper from his coat pocket and smoothed it out on Gideon's back.

'Found this pinned to his shirt. Some writing on it.'

'What's it say?'

'Can't read.'

'Give it here.'

Josiah handed over the piece of paper.

'Keep that light steady, will you,' the man chided, peering at the faint writing. 'It's faded some, but see that?' He pointed. 'That word says RUSTLER. That there is a name. It's not clear, but I'd guess it says Joseph Crane.'

Josiah craned his neck. 'Who?' he asked.

'Joseph Crane.'

'Never heard of 'im.'

'Me neither,' said the man, squinting at Josiah. 'Lynched you say?'

'Yep.'

'Best take him to the sheriff.'

'Pa! You said we was gonna sell it.'

'Shut up.'

'What did he say?' asked the man.

'Nothin'. Take no notice of 'im.' With his index finger Josiah made a twirling motion at the side of his temple. 'He's a bit on the slow side. Stupid like.'

'I ain't stupid, Pa.'

'Yes you are.' To the man with the lantern he added, 'Gets it from his ma's side of the family.'

'Ma weren't stupid, Pa.'

'She was so.'

'Stupid enough to marry you, eh, Pa?'

Josiah's fist thumped the back of his son's head.

Silenced, Jebadiah went into a sulk, muttering under his breath.

Seeing the money he'd hoped to raise disappearing fast Josiah decided to adopt the persona of a good citizen.

'Yes, let's go see the sheriff,' he said resignedly.

The man grabbed the lantern. 'It's this way,' he said, beckoning the trio to follow.

'Come on, boys,' Josiah said sadly.

A light from the window of the sheriff's office cast a yellow glow on the boardwalk and street. The man knocked the door loudly before opening it.

'Sheriff,' he called out. 'Got a dead body out here.'

Sheriff Wade stepped out from behind his desk and followed the man into the street. The man held out the piece of paper.

'This was pinned to his chest. Says his name is Joseph Crane, and that he's a rustler. Those fellows,' he pointed, 'found him hanging from a tree.'

At the sheriff's behest Josiah told what had happened.

'Bring him over to Doc Thomas,' said Sheriff Wade, and he led the way.

The body was laid out on a wooden bench in a shed at the back of the doctor's house. Doc Thomas officially pronounced him dead. Death caused by strangulation.

'He wouldn't have died quick,' he commented, examining the rope Josiah handed over. 'Simple slipknot. Not very humane,' he added. 'Copeland's land, eh?'

The sheriff looked quizzically at the physician. 'What, Doc?'

'Copeland's land. Where they found him.'

'Yeah. I'll have him buried. Unmarked grave.'

3

'We lost more beeves last night, boss.' Jez Moxley balanced his Stetson hat on one finger, 'Tex said there's no sign of the bunch he'd pushed north of the river.'

Henry Copeland smashed his big fist on the top of his green-leather-topped desk.

'When?'

Moxley frowned questioningly. 'When did he push 'em, or when did he find they were missing?'

Copeland drew in a lungful of smoke. 'Both.'

'Week or so ago. Probably in Mexico now.'

The rancher stubbed out the cigar he had been enjoying until the interruption. 'How many?'

'More'n twenty head, Tex reckons.' Moxley was determined to retain the trust of his employer, but in truth the count had been double that number.

Copeland slammed down his fist a second time. 'That's more than fifty this month.'

Moxley shrugged. 'Want me to round up some of the boys?'

Copeland looked at him as if he was stupid. 'And do

what exactly? he demanded, getting to his feet. 'You'll never find them. Like you say, they're probably well inside Mexico by now.' He sat down heavily. 'Get back to work. I need time to think.'

The ramrod put on his hat and left his boss to his contemplation. Once outside, on the front porch of the sprawling ranch house, he stretched out his arms and yawned, smiling inwardly at the cunning of his deception. For years he and his henchmen had made a tidy profit running off Copeland's cattle. Most of them they drove across the border into Mexico, after altering the brand to that of Moxley's partner, Zebulon Grant – changing the Bar C to the Triple-Bar 8 was easy. Grant owned a small spread bordering the eastern boundary of Copeland's huge ranch.

So far Copeland had demonstrated no suspicion of who was actually responsible for rustling his beeves. But every now and then Moxley would finger some unknown drifter who made the mistake of being caught crossing Bar C land. Moxley made certain that none of those he caught was allowed to say much, then encouraged Copeland to hang every one he caught as a warning against rustling his cattle. To date Copeland had hanged four drifters.

After his foreman had left, Copeland got up from his desk and for several minutes he stared out of the window at the distant blue hills. Then he returned to his leather-padded chair, closed his eyes and slumped back in his seat. A few steers here and there was no great loss, but this rustling was getting out of hand. Losing around fifty head a month was beginning to put a strain on his previously unhindered cash flow. He realized that the time had come for him to do something about it. But what exactly? He hadn't yet figured out the answer to that question.

Up till last year Moxley had seemed well able to handle any problem that had arisen. He'd kept on top of wandering homesteaders, Indians, raiding Mexican bandits, yes, and rustlers. But now something had changed. Was Moxley getting too old to cut the mustard? He must be over thirty-five, H.J. thought, maybe pushing forty.

The ramrod had worked for the Copeland family for over twenty years, arriving as a thirteen- or fourteen-year-old snot-nosed orphan kid, a year before H.J's widowed father had died. Jez had grown up tall and mean, strong as a bull. A man of action who didn't suffer fools. Promoting the tough cowhand to foreman had not been difficult. Moxley had soon imposed himself upon the bunkhouse rats.

Copeland wrestled with his problems, elbows on the desk, head in his hands. At forty-eight years old, he had begun to realize just how lonely his life had become. Fifteen years earlier he had lost his first wife and two infant boys to an influenza epidemic that had nearly taken his own life. Becky had been the love of his life. He wasn't prone to bouts of nostalgia, but now, just thinking about her brought him close to crying. He had achieved everything he had set out to, and more. He had taken over a modest sized ranch from his father, and had developed it into the largest outfit in the territory.

The more he contemplated, the more restless he felt, the more unhappy he became. He was rich beyond his wildest dreams, the biggest landowner, the richest, the most powerful. He owned the bank, livery, general stores.

28

Heck; he owned the whole town of Prospect Falls. When H.J. sneezed, the entire area caught a cold: the mayor and town council, the sheriff, the judge. Copeland owned them all. But despite all his power and influence he was not content. And now some rogue band of desperadoes was rustling his beef, big time.

The chair scraped back on the highly polished wooden floorboards as he stood abruptly, a monumental decision made; he would buy himself some new muscle, a strong, ruthless enforcer, a man with a proven reputation for fixing the problems of rich men. All he had to do was find such a man, or men. He decided to go into town next morning to speak to some people. He would start with his lawyer and see where that led.

After nearly 200 miles of hard riding, through countless towns and settlements, and still with no news of young Joey Crane, Matt Walker and Bob Crane reached the San Carlos valley in southern New Mexico. Both men were weary, both had begun to question the effectuality of the quest they had pledged themselves to.

The search moved on, but still they found no one who remembered Joey or seeing a young man fitting his description, and when Las Cruces proved to be a hopeless washout, Matt's vexation grew to an intolerable level.

'We're not getting anywhere with this.' Matt's frustration was obvious.

Bob pulled a face. 'Maybe we should go about it by coming at it from the opposite direction.'

Matt looked quizzically at his brother-in-law. 'Like what?'

'Like, how about we start at Odessa and work our way back to Sweetwater Springs?'

'But we might find something in the next place we come to.'

'I seem to recall you sayin' that on at least three occasions.'

'Maybe you're right,' Matt conceded. 'What exactly you got in mind?'

'Take the train south to El Paso, then another up to Odessa,' Bob suggested. 'That's where Joey told his mother he planned to leave the train, isn't it? From Odessa we can ride the trail to Sweetwater Springs, taking Joey's most likely route.'

The two men chewed over the pros and cons for a while, and in the end Matt agreed with Bob's proposed change of plan.

The carriages on the Pacific and Southern Railroad were still very new, and the train journey proved to be very agreeable with the comfortable quilted seating. It was most definitely faster and less tiring than travelling on horseback, despite the more roundabout route.

Joey had wired his mother from Odessa, telling her that he had enjoyed his trip so far, and that he had met a lot of nice people of diverse backgrounds on the trains, and that he was now looking forward to the ride to Arizona. He had been most taken with the relief conductor on the train, a certain Mr Moore, who was actually the depot manager in Odessa. A kindly man, he had written, who had offered much in the way of advice.

The train journey was uneventful. Bob slept most of the

way, and after retrieving their horses Matt and Bob sought out the depot manager.

Harry Moore greeted them warmly. Yes, he remembered the well-mannered young man.

'Remember him well,' he said with much affection. 'Reminded me of my middle son,' he told them. 'Helped me quieten down a rowdy passenger. A drunken cowboy who was annoying the other travellers, particularly the ladies. I remember it all despite it being quite a few weeks ago,' he reflected. 'Joey sent his mother a wire. A lovely polite young man. Told me his plan was to take a horseback ride from Odessa to Arizona to stay with his Uncle Matt. Oh! Sorry,' he apologized, 'that's you, isn't it?'

Matt nodded. 'Please continue.'

'Well, when he told me his plan, I advised him to have a rethink, telling him that he was taking on nearly three hundred miles of painful riding that he didn't need to. I recall him listening intently before saying he still intended to make the journey on horseback, but that he would accept my suggestion to rejoin the train and stay on until it reached El Paso.'

'So he didn't get off the train in Odessa?'

'Well, he did, but only until the train got going again. There was a small problem with the locomotive, took about an hour to get it working correctly. I said goodbye to him at El Paso.' He gave a curt nod to emphasize what he had told them.

Matt gave Bob a sideways glance. 'So we're starting from the wrong place?'

Mr Moore shrugged apologetically. 'I am afraid so.'

'When's the next train to El Paso?'

Mr Moore took out his railway watch. 'In about two hours.'

'Thanks. Is there a cantina or saloon round here where we can get something to eat?'

Mr Moore smiled. 'Yes. Oscar Hernandez and his lovely wife, Rosa, have a cantina about half a mile east of here.' He pointed a finger. 'Follow that track, you can't miss it. Used to be a stage-line depot.'

Matt thanked Mr Moore for his time and said goodbye.

Bob watched the railroad official walk away, then took off his hat and wiped the sweat from his face and neck with a red handkerchief.

'What a waste of time, eh? Sorry.'

Matt shrugged. 'You weren't to know Joey changed his plan and stayed on the train.'

Bob turned on his heel. 'Maybe we should have stayed with our original plan,' he said as he walked away to where the horses were hitched.

Oscar Hernandez's cantina was really a large shack with a corral at the back. They ate a bowl of fiery bean stew, which the owner of the cantina swore contained chicken. Neither Bob nor Matt found the slightest trace of any kind of bird – not even a feather – but at least it was tasty and filling.

The two men joked on the way back to the railroad depot.

'Kinda bird you reckon it was?' asked Matt. 'A phantom bird?'

'Cluck, cluck!' Bob replied with a belly-laugh.

The meal at least provided a touch of humour to an otherwise serious situation.

The train was bang on time. Horses loaded, Matt and Bob settled down for the trip back to El Paso.

As soon as they reached the town Matt wired his sister to tell her what had happened and to bring her up to speed with their progress, also asking if she had heard from Joey. After that he wired Ed Massey to ask if Joey had turned up in Sweetwater Springs. Then, tired and weary, they headed for the quietest hotel they could find.

El Paso had gained a notorious reputation as a lawless gun-town, frequented by gunslingers and outlaws. Matt and Bob both agreed that they wanted to steer well clear of any troublemakers. The hotel they chose was a pretty, whitewashed two storey building displaying the word TEM-PERANCE on its name plaque. It had a small dining room exclusive to guests of the hotel. The middle-aged woman who ran the place was a sour-faced witch, who didn't appear to have one ounce of human kindness in her whole being, but her hotel suited their purpose perfectly.

Next morning they called at the telegraph office situated at the rail depot. Matt's sister had sent a reply. Joey had not made any kind of contact. The news from Ed was no better.

4

Calling it a road was a big exaggeration, thought Matt as they rode west into the afternoon sun. The surface of the track was deeply rutted, with many holes waiting to trap a horse's hoof. Matt tried to recall if he had seen rain clouds over this way when they had passed north of where they were now. He mentioned it to Bob.

'Must have been a heavy storm when we were on the train,' Bob drawled.

'Seems likely,' Matt agreed.

Around three-quarters of the way to Prospect Falls it began to grow dark; the absence of light made it too hard to be sure of dodging the potholes, and the undulating range on either side of the road, littered with brush and boulders, wasn't an alternative. Added to which, a light rain began to fall.

'Need to find a place to hole up,' Bob said casually.

In the distance the dim lights of a small settlement shone welcomingly. The closer they got the more welcoming the sight became. They headed their horses in that

34

direction with a renewed vigour.

'What did you say the name of this place was?' Matt asked as they rode past a couple of adobe buildings.

'Valdes. According to the map. We passed about thirty miles north of here on our outward journey,' Bob replied as the rain stopped. 'Hopefully there'll be a cantina. Probably won't be any kind of hotel, or accommodation, so we'll likely be lucky to find any place better than a stable to bed down.'

'At least we might get a drink,' said Matt.

'You hope.'

Two rows of adobes with whitewashed walls were spaced out along a rutted track that passed for the main street. Hitching the horses outside the only building showing a light, Bob pushed aside the patterned blanket that served as the door, and stepped inside, rifle under one arm, saddle-bags across the other. The interior of the tiny cantina was dark, the air pungent, heavy with the stink of tallow candles and sweat.

The swarthy-skinned owner greeted them cheerfully with a broad smile across a wide mouth filled to capacity with gleaming white teeth. 'Welcome, *señores*. What is your desire?'

Bob Crane dumped his saddle-bag and Winchester on a chair and leaned one elbow on the rough-sawn plank of wood that served for a bar.

'What you got?'

The *dueño* grinned, '*Mezcal*. Good.'

'Got any whiskey?'

'Sorry, *señor*, alas no whiskey. Maybe I can find some tequila, yes?'

Bob turned to face his travelling companion, hip-cocked as he leaned against the bar. 'Matt? Tequila?'

Matt nodded.

'Tequila it is, *dueño.*'

'*Sí, señor,* I fetch it. Please,' he gestured, 'take a seat.'

'*Dueño?*' Matt queried.

'It means bar owner,' Bob explained. 'Is there a livery stable?' he called out to the *dueño.*

'Alas no, *señor.* But you can put your horses in my stable if you want. It is at the back.'

'Thanks. Can we bed down there for the night?'

'*Sí, señor.*' he held out a hand, palm up. 'One Yankee dollar,' he shrugged and smiled. 'Each,' he added quickly.

Both Americans laughed as Matt handed over the money. The *dueño* lit a lantern and handed it over. Bob took it and went off to stable the horses.

While Bob was away Matt heard horses outside, then a tall, superbly dressed Mexican strode confidently into the cantina, silver spurs chinking loudly. His black tailored suit, edged with silver and white piping, was patterned with gems that reflected the light from the candles. The sound of his black knee-length riding boots was loud the wooden floorboards. On his hips sat a pair of ivory-andled pistols set in beautiful holsters that hung from a finely tooled black and silver gunbelt. A wide-brimmed black-and-silver patterned sombrero crowned the man's head.

The Mexican looked over the bar. Seeing no one, he rapped on the surface with a short black leather riding-rop. 'Pedro!' he called out, 'Tequila. *Pronto.*'

The *dueño* scurried back through a curtain made of

patterned beads. He was carrying two bottles. He spoke in Spanish.

'My apologies, *patron*,' he grovelled, knuckling his fore-head, almost letting one of the bottles fall from his grasp.

'Tequila!' ordered the tall Mexican, obviously not happy at having to bother repeating himself. For added effect, he hammered the riding crop on the bar.

The *dueño* dusted off both bottles, then fetched a clean cloth and wiped out a glass. He drew the cork of one bottle with a lively pop, and with one hand behind his back, poured out a measure. '*Patron*,' he grovelled.

The tall Mexican tapped the riding crop on the bar twice. The *dueño* stared for a moment until the light went on in his brain.

'A thousand apologies, *patron*,' he said in Spanish, turning to the counter behind him, returning with a dish of sliced lemon and a small terracotta bowl filled with salt.

Matt watched the one-act play with interest. It was obvious that the newcomer was a man of importance. The Mexican removed one fine black-leather glove and licked the skin of his thumb and forefinger, sprinkling a pinch of salt where he had licked. Next he gripped a piece of lemon between thumb and forefinger, and grasped the tequila in his gloved hand. He breathed out, licked the salt, then downed the shot glass of tequila in one gulp, fin-ishing the ritual by biting the lemon.

He set down the glass. 'Another,' he ordered in Spanish.

The *dueño* flashed a broad smile of approval and poured out a second glassful, knuckling his forehead, before setting down the bottle.

Bob came back in and sat down wearily. He saw Matt's

amused expression.

'What's up?' he asked.

Matt nodded his head towards the tall Mexican as the *dueño* hurried over to their table with a tray containing a bottle of tequila, two shot glasses, salt and slices of lemon.

'*Señores*,' he said, setting down the tray, 'please enjoy.'

He scurried back behind the bar, turning abruptly as three more Mexicans entered. From their dress, Matt took them to be working *vaqueros*.

The tall Mexican also turned.

'*Patron*,' the larger framed newcomer said, removing his sombrero.

The tall Mexican beckoned to them. '*Bienvenido, Luiz. Ven a tomar una copa. Ustedes también, Pedro, Jose.*'

Matt nudged Bob's elbow. 'What did he say?' he whispered.

Bob's answer was also whispered. 'The tall guy welcomed them. Asked them to come have a drink.'

'Oh.'

The other two Mexicans removed their sombreros, and bowed their heads. They moved respectfully to the bar.

'Tequila,' the tall Mexican commanded in a voice that was used to being obeyed without question.

The large vaquero bowed, and answered in Spanish. 'Thank you, *patron*. We would prefer mezcal.' The other three nodded.

Matt nudged Bob again, a quizzical look on his face.

'He offered tequila, they said they preferred mezcal.'

The tall Mexican turned to the *dueño*. 'We will sit,' he announced in Spanish, glancing around the room.

'*Sí, patron.*' the *dueño* looked nervously across at Matt and Bob.

'*Mi mesa de siempre,*' the tall Mexican added.

'Oh-oh!' Bob exclaimed.

'What's the matter?' Matt asked.

'The boss man said he wants to sit at his usual table. I guess it's this one.'

At his boss's command Luiz clicked his heels. In Spanish he said, 'I will see to it, *patron.*' He crammed his sombrero on to his head and marched over to Matt and Bob's table.

Bob gestured towards the *vaquero.* 'This guy says he's going to fix it.'

The *vaquero* spoke softly in broken English.

'Excuse me, gringos. My apologies. It is unfortunate, but you will have to move.'

Bob Crane looked deep into the *vaquero*'s brown eyes. 'Say what?'

The Mexican's face stiffened. '*Señor.* It is with great regret, but you will have to move.'

Bob looked across at Matt for support. Matt nodded.

'*Señor,*' Bob spoke quietly, '*vete a la mierda,*' he said in fluent Spanish.

The *vaquero*'s flashing smile turned swiftly, his eyes narrowed at the rudeness of the gringo's insult, the corners of his mouth turned down.

'You don't understand, gringo. This is the table of my patron. You must move.'

Bob gestured around the tiny cantina. 'Plenty of room. You choose.'

The *vaquero*'s right hand moved casually down to his

side, flipping the rawhide thong from the hammer of his side-iron.

'You don't understand,' he repeated.

'No. *You* don't understand,' Bob shouted, kicking back the chair in one sudden movement that ended when his huge right fist smashed into the *vaquero*'s face. Blood spurted as the Mexican's head banged on to the floor – he was out cold.

Another of the *vaqueros* made to go for his six-gun, until the metallic sound of the hammer on Matt's Colt clicking back stopped him in his tracks.

'I wouldn't do that if I were you,' Matt called out.

Bob massaged his knuckles and translated. '*Yo no lo haria eso si fuera tu.*'

The tall Mexican stepped forward, a faint smile of amusement on his lips. He placed a hand on that of the would-be gunslinger.

'Stay calm, Jose,' he said.

To Bob he said in Spanish. 'You speak our language well, gringo.' His confident voice was even and measured. 'My man only sought to please me,' he continued, now in fluent English. 'That is the table where I usually sit.' He pointed. 'It is of no great importance.'

He swished his riding crop at a fly that buzzed too close. 'Allow me to introduce myself. My name is Don Hector Juan-Carlos Cervantes de Lopez-Castro. This cantina, this village, are part of my estate.'

'How far does your estate extend?'

'On this side of the border it includes most of this county plus large parts of the two adjacent counties. In Mexico it stretches from the Rio Bravo, you gringos know it as the Rio Grande, almost to the city of Chihuahua.'

'Won't you join us?' Matt invited, liking the tall Mexican instantly. He watched the other *vaqueros* lift their colleague up and set him on a chair. The dueño splashed water on the vaquero's face till he came round. Don Hector smiled and nodded.

'With pleasure,' he said pulling out a chair. The *dueño* hurried over with another shot glass. 'May I enquire what brings you to this place?'

Matt took the tintype from his shirt pocket.

'This is my . . sorry . . *our* nephew, Joey Crane,' he said, handing it to Don Hector. He was riding to visit me in Arizona, but he has gone missing. We are searching for him.' He explained who they were. 'We believe he came this way.'

Don Hector swivelled in his chair, and spoke in English. 'Pedro. Did this young Americano pass through the village?' He held up the picture.

The *dueño* almost ran across the room to his patron. A smile of recognition appeared on his face when he looked at the tintype.

'*Sí, patron,*' he affirmed. 'I saw him. It was weeks ago. I gave him water. He told me he was heading to Mesilla and then for the gringo town at Prospect Falls.'

'Which route did he take?'

'Directly west, *patron.*'

Don Hector nodded knowingly. 'The Bar C,' he said softly. 'Copeland's land.' He grimaced and shook his head.

'We've heard about the Bar C. Biggest ranch in the territory, isn't it?' said Matt.

'*Sí.* It is big. Almost as big as mine.' Don Hector looked pensive. 'I have heard many stories about *Señor* Copeland and his men. My *vaqueros* have had many, how you say, run-ins with Copeland's men. Anyone travelling across his land must take care. There are many rumours.' He smiled. 'Anyway, it is growing late. My men and I have been on the range for several days, and I very am hungry.'

He stood up abruptly. 'Please gather up your things. Tonight you will be guests at my hacienda. My mother, Doña Maria, and my sister, Elena, are with me at the rancheria,' he added. 'They will be pleased to meet you. We have not so many visitors these days.'

When Matt made to protest, Don Hector raised a hand. 'I will take no refusal. *Mi casa es su casa.*' He bowed then turned. 'Luiz, Pedro. *Vete a buscar los caballos.*'

Matt looked at Bob. 'He told them to fetch our horses,' said Bob.

Minutes later Don Hector was leading the group of horsemen the ten or so miles to his hacienda.

5

The lights of Rancho Castro loomed out of the dark prairie as the little cavalcade approached. Torches flared as men rushed out to take care of the horses.

Don Hector led the way up a flight of three stone steps to the covered veranda at the front of a magnificent house. Lanterns burned brightly, whitewashed walls reflecting the light. Hector took off his sombrero and opened one of the double doors. Stepping to one side, he ushered Matt and Bob inside. A tall woman dressed in black appeared at another doorway. In one hand she carried a fan.

'Hector.' She smiled lovingly; her voice sounded warm and cultured.

'Mother,' Hector replied in Spanish. He crossed the room to meet her. 'I have brought home two guests to meet you. Americanos.' He gestured towards Bob and Matt.

The woman fluttered her fan for a split second, then said, 'You are most welcome, *señores*.' She slipped the fan into a pocket and clapped her hands loudly. 'Lanterns,'

43

she called out.

From various doorways servants appeared carrying lanterns and candelabras, and in seconds the room was as bright as day. The now well-lit room was sumptuously furnished.

'Where is Elena?' Hector asked. 'I want her to meet our guests.'

The sound of light footsteps on the stairs heralded the arrival of a beautiful and excited young woman. Elegantly dressed, she was truly beautiful, with a rich olive complexion, delicately tinted cheeks and full red lips which, when parted, revealed teeth of dazzling whiteness. Her large brown eyes seemed capable of a great depth of expression.

She danced into the room and threw her arms around Hector's neck, kissing him on both cheeks.

Hector took her hand. 'Elena. We have guests.' He nodded towards Matt and Bob.

Elena made a slight bow with her head, raising the elaborately embroidered fan in front of her slightly flushed face, her long eyelashes fluttering in time with the fan. Her breath caught in her throat at the sight of the tall stranger who stood holding his hat in both hands, a nervous smile on his lips.

'*Señores*,' she gushed, her sweet voice almost breathless.

Her hands were small and shapely, and her form was willowy and lissom. Matt was immediately captivated.

Hector's guests were wined and dined royally. After dinner, over a glass of brandy, Hector leaned his elbows on the table.

'*Amigos*, I have a proposition I should like to put to

you.' He steepled his hands, touching his clean-shaven chin with his fingertips, eyeing the interested expressions on the faces of his two guests.

'After you have found your nephew I would like you both to come and work for me.' He held up a hand to still a response. 'I need someone to manage the American part of my estate. As I believe I have already mentioned, my main home is across the border in Chihuahua; this *estancia* was once the home of my mother's family. You would have complete control.'

His brown eyes searched for a positive reaction. 'You would be well rewarded,' he added. 'Salary plus a share of the profits. What do you say?' He leaned back in his chair and took a sip of brandy.

For a moment Matt was dumbstruck. Don Hector's proposal came as a complete surprise. He shot a glance in Bob's direction. Bob just shrugged. Matt recovered his composure.

'Hector. You do us a great honour,' Matt said, and added: 'A tempting offer, but I know little about cattle, or running a ranch. I don't think Bob knows much either.' Bob shook his head gently from side to side.

Hector pressed on: 'That would not be a problem. Luiz, my *segundo*, will take care of the cattle side of the business. No, I need one or two strong men such as yourselves to be the *patrón*. Organize shipments. Ensure that rustling is keep to a minimum. Make sure Copeland's men keep away from *our*,' he gestured, 'cattle.'

'Hector, I'm not sure I – we,' Matt corrected, 'could handle it.'

Hector shook his head. 'I pride myself that I am a good

judge of character, and in my opinion you have all the necessary qualities. Intelligence. Determination. Honesty.' He ticked each one off on his fingers. 'Added to your vast experience in maintaining law and order.' He smiled. 'Bob, you are tempted, no?'

Bob shrugged. '*Sí*, I am tempted.'

'Look, sleep on it. Consider carefully what I have said. Discuss all the pros and cons. You will see there are many more pros than cons. In less than ten years you would be rich men. Men of great influence and importance. It is the chance of a lifetime.'

Matt held up his hands in mock surrender. 'OK,' he agreed. 'We will discuss, consider, and sleep on it.'

'It is my fervent wish that you will accept.'

'Hector, you are a very persuasive man. You do us a great honour.'

'Good. One more brandy to celebrate our happy meeting. And our future together. OK?'

The two Americans smiled and nodded.

'Let's not jump the gun, Hector,' Matt cautioned.

Hector's face split into a broad grin. 'OK.' He took out a leather cigar case. 'May I offer you a cigar?' Bob took one. Matt declined.

Hector looked across the table at his guests. 'You are indeed fortunate to be here. Tonight we are holding a small celebration in honour of a girl and boy from the *estancia* who are getting married tomorrow. There will be music, dancing, feasting and of course much alcohol.' He looked at the big grandfather clock standing against the wall opposite. 'The celebrations will commence in an hour or so, which gives us time to finish our cigars and brandy.'

Matt smiled. 'Hector. If you and Bob don't mind, I'll leave you and take a turn outside.'

'Of course.'

Matt left Hector and Bob to their cigars and walked into the cool air of the spacious hallway. There he drew up sharply in surprise: Elena was standing at the open doorway of the drawing room. She flashed an encouraging smile in his direction.

'Will you walk with me, Matt?'

Matt was surprised by her invitation. 'Yes, of course,' he said, regaining his composure.

Elena smiled again. 'I will get my shawl.'

On the wide veranda they stood for a moment, looking at the bright moon and the distant hills lit by the afterglow of the sun.

'Tell me more about yourself,' she said.

Matt turned to face her. He gazed into her dark eyes, sparkling in the lantern light, which also brought a golden glow to her silky skin. Elena was more beautiful than he had realized.

Dutifully, he told her of his life, and again about the quest he and Bob were engaged upon. He found her easy to talk to, and that he was eager to tell her everything.

'Did I hear you say that you were leaving in the morning?'

'Yes. Bob and I plan to make an early start.'

'Perhaps we will meet again soon. I wish for it.'

Matt took her hand in his. 'I sincerely hope so,' he said softly, raising her hand to his lips, and planting a kiss.

Burning embers leaped skywards as the flames from more

than a dozen bonfires lit up the night sky. Dark shadows of breathless dancers flitted across the walls of the adobe buildings surrounding the yard. The sound of music and laughter filled the air; the merriment was a joy to behold. The guests stood in a wide circle surrounding the dancers, moving back and forth in waves of delight, their faces bathed in the glow of the fires.

Standing next to Elena, Matt felt his foot tapping instinctively on the hard-baked earth in time with the music. Bob had set down his glass of tequila and was clapping, his hands almost a blur of movement. He joined in with his deep voice to the many shouts of encouragement to the dancers.

As the rhythms of the music grew ever more lively the dancers slipped away to join the crowd leaving the betrothed couple alone in the centre of the circle. The boy was dressed in white and had an expression of serious concentration on his handsome sunburned face. The girl wore a white blouse and flowing crimson skirt, which she raised above her knees as she stamped her foot down, revealing a smooth and shapely brown leg. She moved gracefully, constantly brushing provocatively against her intended, flashing a smile of white teeth, a coquettish expression returning as she flickered her eyelashes, taunting, teasing.

'*Ole! Ole!*' the girl chanted repeatedly; the excited crowd answered with the same cry. Suddenly the musicians quickened the tempo until the music reached its climax. The lovers embraced, then kissed to loud applause and yells of encouragement from the crowd. Many surged forward to engulf the couple amidst rounds of back-slapping and hugging. The couple and their friends retreated to the refreshment table as the band resumed its playing in a slower tempo, guitars strumming rhythmically, crisp notes from the solitary trumpet piercing the night air.

Matt felt a touch on his arm and turned. Elena smiled a captivating smile.

'Dance with me, Matt?'

He was a little embarrassed at her words; he had always considered that he possessed two left feet.

'I'm not sure I know how,' he said truthfully.

'It is not difficult. I will instruct you.' She took his hand and led him to the centre of the circle. 'Do as I do,' she instructed. Her eyes flashed in the firelight, shining with an intensity to rival any flame.

With a delicate arm around his waist, Elena lifted the hem of her skirt, and placed one foot alongside Matt's, allowing him a sight of a slim ankle. Her body swayed gracefully as she encouraged him to follow her. She stepped with an exaggerated sway of her hips, each sensual movement compelling his gaze. He repeated the steps as best he could, but more clumsily. Their bodies came together, their arms entwined as she twirled him around.

All too soon the dance ended, leaving Matt breathless, not from the physical effort but from being in such close proximity to such a radiant beauty. Elena curtsied, her skirt spread wide as she dipped her head toward Matt. He bowed in as dignified manner as he could; this was the first time he had ever bowed and he felt awkward as his face flushed with embarrassment.

The crowd burst into a round of spontaneous applause, raising Matt's level of embarrassment even further; he hadn't realized people had been watching.

Elena smiled. 'Thank you, Matt, that was most enjoyable. You are a much better dancer that you admitted to.'

Matt frowned. 'I'm certain you are exaggerating, Elena, but I thank you.'

She gave his arm a squeeze. 'You are too modest. But now I must leave you. I will return soon.' With that she threw her shawl over her shoulder, turned on her heel and walked slowly away, pausing here and there to exchange greetings with other guests.

Matt watched her with eyes like a hawk, loving the rhythmic sway of her hips as she moved, not wanting to miss one poetic movement. He went off to find Bob, knowing that Elena had captivated his heart.

'He is handsome, no?' Doña Maria said in Spanish.

'Who is?'

'Do not try to be coy, Elena. You know very well who I mean.'

Elena looked down at her fan, inspecting the lace edging.

'Well? Answer me. Is he not handsome?'

Elena tried to sound matter of fact. 'I had not noticed.'

'And,' added Doña Maria, 'he is the perfect gentleman. His manners are faultless.'

'*Sí*,' Elena shrugged, 'perhaps.'

Doña Maria's eyes flashed irritatedly. 'Sometimes, Elena, you have the ability to make me so very angry.'

Elena felt the piercing gaze of her mother's eyes cut through her defences. She shuffled uncomfortably in her seat, unable to escape her mother's stare. Eventually she felt obliged to give in and answer. 'OK, Mother. *Sí*, he is handsome, with exemplary manners.'

'Ha!' exclaimed Doña Maria. That one syllable said it all.

In the cool dark shadows of the stables Matt Walker was tightening the cinch strap around his horse. Bob had already led the two packhorses and his mount into the bright sunlight. They had breakfasted on ham and eggs; the taste still remained, along with the appetizing smell of freshly baked bread.

'Don't make it too tight.' Elena's soft voice startled him.

Matt turned. She stood a few feet away from him, a shaft of sunlight reflected from a window high up bathed her face. She was so very beautiful.

'I wanted to say my farewell in private,' she said, stepping towards him. Her lips parted as she raised herself on to tiptoe. Instinctively he bent his face toward hers. There was no mistaking the passion that Elena packed into that one long sensual kiss.

When he opened his eyes she was gone.

6

On the way to Mesilla the brothers-in-law decided to split up to check out a couple of tiny settlements. They agreed on a spot and a time to meet up later.

Matt Walker lay on his back in the warm grass at the side of a trickling stream, staring up at blue cloudless sky, waiting for Bob. Flies buzzed annoyingly, interrupting his moment of solitude. His head was filled with happy thoughts of Elena and their all too brief moment of tenderness. Overhead, birds wheeled high in the sky. Tiny beads of sweat formed on his head, making his scalp itch irritatingly. He smoothed a hand through his hair, scratching at the offending spot. 'Need a haircut,' he said under his breath, listening to the cracking of the grass around him. The long stalk of grass that had tasted so sweet when he had first plucked it had now gone limp and tasteless. He squinted at the sun, and pushed himself up on to one elbow, tossing away the grass stalk.

Bob Crane's deep voice shattered the silence, snapping him from his thoughts.

'Find out anything?'

'No. You?' Matt asked.

'Nothing.'

Bob stepped down for a few minutes, took a drink of water from his canteen, then refilled the bottle from the stream.

'Come on. Let's get going.'

The horses were rested, snorting to each other to indicate they were ready to be off.

'I was thinking,' said Bob, as they jogged along the track.

'Careful, *amigo*.'

'I'm not joking, Matt. I think we should maybe return to Sweetwater Springs. We aren't getting anywhere.'

Matt shot him a glance. 'Bob. I'm not ready to give up yet. I promised my sister I'd find Joey. I'm sure we're getting closer to finding him. I don't know why, I just sort of feel it. I'm certain we'll find something soon.' He saw Bob's sceptical expression. 'Tell you what. Let's check out Mesilla and Prospect Falls; then if nothing turns up we'll head back. What do you say?'

After thinking over the proposal for a few minutes Bob agreed.

They made camp that night near a fast-flowing river.

Matt sipped his hot coffee. The silence broken only by the crackling of dry sticks and logs on the campfire. He glanced sideways at his brother-in-law.

'It's been a few years since we last met. What have you been up to?'

Bob Crane seemed surprised by the sharpness of Matt's question. 'Scouting for the army mostly,' he replied.

'Riding dispatch for various generals. Stuff like that. Why?'

'Just curious. See much action?'

'Some.'

Matt remembered that Bob Crane had always been a man of few words.

'What about you? Figurin' on stayin' with the law?' Bob asked.

'I might,' answered Matt. 'For a while yet, maybe. I've a hankerin' to get me a small ranch in a couple of years from now.'

'In New Mexico?'

'No. Figure North California would be better. We'll see,' he shrugged. 'I've been offered a good job with the Pinkertons, running their operation in that area. Might give that a go for a while, or maybe accept a job with the railroad, organizing their security. They keep askin'. Might even start my own investigation business. Either way, every one of those options pay better than being a town marshal.'

Bob perked up at what Matt had said. 'Sounds a mighty interestin' prospect,' he commented. 'Maybe I'll come in with you.'

'Maybe I'll ask you,' Matt snorted.

'What did you make of Hector's proposal?'

Matt looked at him thoughtfully. 'I don't know. It's a tempting offer. What about you?'

'Sounded like the best idea I'd heard in years. Needs serious consideration.' Bob laughed out loud. 'More coffee?'

Matt held out his tin cup. 'Why not?' he said.

*

The ride to Mesilla proved to be profitable. In each of the three small settlements they rode through that day people confirmed having seen a young man answering to Joey's description. Two said they remembered meeting him. All said he had told them he was on his way to Prospect Falls by way of Mesilla.

Mesilla was a vibrant, sprawling town, much larger than Matt or Bob had been led to believe. At the Mexican end of town was a tightly packed area of grey/white adobe houses, with colourful strings of red peppers hanging at the side of each door to dry. Broad-hipped women with dark complexions were gathered around a well, chattering loudly as they waited their turn to draw water. Little bare-footed children ran around noisily. It was a happy scene.

The buildings in the centre of town were mostly of rough-sawn timber construction. New buildings were springing up everywhere.

First stop was the town sheriff's office. The aged lawman remembered seeing a young man ride through some weeks earlier, but couldn't recall him stopping off anywhere.

'Remember his horse though,' he said in a broad Southern drawl. 'Big sorrel with three white stockings. Fine-looking animal; looked fast.'

The sheriff confirmed that there were a number of small ranches thereabouts, and also two big ones. One, the Bar C, was owned by a wealthy rancher by the name of H.J. Copeland.

'A good man,' he added. 'Strong, but fair. Does a lot for the local community. His spread stretches for miles. From here to and beyond Prospect Falls.' His florid complexion glowed. There was a distinctive odour of stale whiskey on his breath.

'We heard some bad reports of this feller Copeland,' Matt told him.

'Bad? No. Copeland's a good man.' The sheriff nodded. 'The other big ranch is some way off to the south, Rancho Castro. Owned by an old Mexican family. It's a bit off the beaten track,' he told them. 'Why don't you check at the livery stable? The young man might have stopped there to buy some feed for that fine-looking horse of his.'

Matt thanked the lawman and the pair headed for the livery stable, a fairly new timber construction, half of it painted dark red. They passed a painter who was stirring a large tin of red paint. They were met at the corral by the owner of the livery stable, a short, tubby man with the rolling gait of a sailor. His two front tobacco-stained teeth, which he sucked almost constantly, protruded a good half-inch from his top lip. He whistled when he spoke, particularly when he pronounced the letter s.

'Yes. I remember him. Nice young feller. Beautiful horse. Asked if he wanted to sell him. Offered good money. Kid turned me down flat.' He looked thoughtful for a moment, then added, 'I remember the brand on the animal. CC it was. That the one?'

'Yes. Joey's father's brand. Charles Crane. Owned a small ranch in Arkansas. This is his brother, Bob Crane.'

'Well, I'm right pleased to meet both of you. Say, while you're here, do you need any feed? Got some top quality oats. Reasonable prices.' He sucked his teeth loudly.

Bob nodded. 'Good idea, sir. We'll take half a bushel.'

'Do you know if Joey stayed here in town?' asked Matt.

'No. I mean yes,' the livery man corrected. 'Your nephew didn't stay. Headed west towards Prospect Falls. Me,' he sniffed, 'I wouldn't have bothered. Don't like the place. Don't like the people. Shifty lot. Rob you as soon as look at you.'

'You seem dead set against the place.'

The tubby man sucked his teeth again. 'Been once. Ain't got no hankerin' to go again.'

'Any specific reason?'

'Don't like the way they do business. The entire place is owned lock stock and barrel by a rancher named Copeland. Henry John,' he added. 'Seems to think he's better than everyone else. Like his shit don't stink, or somethin'. Thinks he owns the whole territory. Wants best quality at tin-pot prices. No sir. I do not desire to do business with such thieves as Henry Copeland.'

'The sheriff told it different,' said Matt.

'How so?'

'Said Copeland was a good man.'

'Amazin' how a few bucks in a man's pocket can alter his opinion, ain't it?' He ran one finger down the side of his nose. 'Like I said, I do not care to do business with such a man as Henry Copeland.'

Matt shrugged in the face of such prejudice, thanked the owner of the livery stable for his help and paid him, while Bob tied the sack of oats to one of the packhorses.

'Take care along that road. There's been a spate of stage hold-ups.'

7

From the other side of the ridge the harsh sound of gunfire echoed around the hills. Matt turned to Bob.

'Shall we take a look?' he asked.

Bob nodded, kicking his horse into a trot. 'Follow me,' he said.

He reined in his horse on the crest of the ridge in a stand of cedars. In the valley below five or six masked bandits were holding up a stagecoach. Bob fished his telescope out of his saddle-bag.

The driver and guard had their hands up, the reins, draped loosely around the brake, hung limply in the still air.

The wheels of the stagecoach creaked and groaned as the team of six horses took a nervous half-step forward, then back. The front and sides of the coach were spattered with red mud dried by the glaring sun.

Three of the passengers, one man and two women, huddled together for support; one of the women was crying. Two other men stood a short distance away. One, a short, squat individual, wore a narrow-brimmed black fedora hat. His business suit was of smooth dark cloth: expensive-looking, it hung well from his corpulent body. A gold watch and chain glinted across the man's vest. Banker? Politician? wondered Bob. Certainly no high-rolling gambler. The man's white shirt and collar looked surprisingly clean. A black bootlace tie completed his attire.

Standing menacingly in front of the man one of the bandits held out a hand, palm extended. In the other he held a Colt, levelled at the man, who was unfastening the watch from his vest. The passenger handed the timepiece over, his face black as thunder. In a high-pitched petulant voice he cursed the robber for a thief and a rogue.

They were the last words he uttered on earth. A single shot rang out, the report echoing along the trail. The man in the black hat reeled backwards, shot through the heart at point-blank range. His lifeless body thumped on to the ground, sending up a tiny cloud of red dust.

Gasps went up from the other passengers; the two women's terrified screams pierced the air. One of them fainted.

Bob raised a hand to shield his eyes from the blazing sun and pointed a finger.

'Want to try the Sharps?' he suggested. 'Think you can hit that murdering devil, then take out a couple more of 'em?'

Without answering the question, Matt dismounted, removed his gloves, and slid the big bore rifle out of its saddle holster.

'Better hurry it up,' said Bob. 'They look like they're getting about ready to leave.'

Matt took off his hat and set it down on a rock, then selected a bullet and pushed it into the chamber; the air was warm on the skin of his ungloved hand. He squinted through the telescopic sight, his mouth suddenly dry, his overactive brain questioning whether he was justified in taking a life. He shrugged away all negative thoughts and tested the strength of the wind with one finger before making a couple of adjustments to the sights. Satisfied, he drew a bead on the nearest mounted bandit and squeezed the trigger.

The shot boomed loud in the still air. Matt repeated the process without waiting to see the result of the shot, confident in his ability as a marksman. Bob watched through his telescope, hearing Matt reload the Sharps. One bandit fell from his horse seconds before Matt aimed at the bandit who had cut down the fat man in black. He fired off a second shot.

'Two down,' Bob whispered as the second man hit the ground. 'The rest of 'em have just realized what's happening.

The other bandits were looking questioningly at one another; their nervous horses skittered and strained on their bridles, aware that something bad was happening. Matt fired again, but this time only winged his target as the bandit spurred his horse into a gallop. His surprised cohorts decided that flight was better than valour and made a run for it.

Matt holstered the Sharps and swung up into the saddle.

Bob led the way down the incline, picking his way around the rocks, trees and bushes on the heavily wooded slope, raising a hand in friendship. The driver raised a hand to return Bob's greeting. The two women cheered loudly. A male passenger whom they hadn't noticed before stumbled out of the coach, knees shaking, thankful to have got through the brief but terrifying ordeal. His eyes were wide, with a vacant look of disbelief.

Bob and Matt reined in near the coach and stepped down. The driver and shotgun guard climbed down from their seat. There was blood on the shoulder of the guard's shirt. The driver tended to the wound.

'Everyone all right?' Bob called out.

'Much obliged to you, mister,' the driver said.

Bob walked over to the body of one of the robbers. He pushed the toe of his boot under the body and flipped the dead man over. Blood still bubbled out between the bandit's gloved fingers; both hands were pressed against his chest where Matt's first bullet had smashed into him.

'Must have still been alive when he hit the ground,' Bob commented, examining the bandit. Matt dragged the second bandit's body over near to the first one. The bandannas covering their faces were pulled away. Bob turned his head.

'Anybody recognize these two?'

The passengers said no without caring to look. The driver and guard bent down to take a closer view.

'I've seen this one before. I think,' the driver said. Then he added quickly, glancing at the guard, 'Ain't he one of them riders used to work for the Bar C?'

The guard took off his sweat-stained hat and scratched his head. After a couple of seconds he nodded.

'Yep. I seen 'im once in town with Jez Moxley.'

'What about the other one?' asked Bob. The driver shook his head slowly from side to side.

'Can't say I ever seen him before.'

'Me neither,' agreed the guard.

The driver looked at Bob. 'By the way, mister, thanks again for what you did. That was sure some fine shootin'.'

The guard too offered his thanks.

'Weren't me,' Bob admitted. 'My partner was the one did the shooting.' He looked over to where Matt was talking to the passengers.

A male passenger was dabbing water on the face of the lady who had fainted.

'She's my wife,' he told Matt.

The passenger who had stumbled out of the coach called out, 'Got any water on this rig?'

The driver ambled back to the coach and reached into the footwell. He tossed a skin of water towards the man. Matt caught it and handed it over. The man swallowed a deep draught, then handed the skin back.

'My wife is inside.' He pointed. 'Would you mind seeing if she wants a drink?'

Matt looked inside the coach. A grey-haired woman of fifty or sixty was slumped unconscious across one of the bench seats. Matt was puzzled – the woman appeared to be old enough to be the man's mother. Her wide-brimmed straw hat lay on the floor of the coach, crumpled, as though it had been stepped upon.

'This woman is unconscious,' Matt called back through the open door.

The man called back. 'She's only fainted. She'll be all right. Splash some water on her face.'

Matt stepped out of the coach. 'You sure like to give out your orders, mister.' He pushed the water-skin into the man's hands. 'You do it,' he commanded, walking away.

Bob stepped over to the body of the passenger who had been shot, the driver and guard followed. He pointed to the fat man.

'He's dead,' he announced, shaking his head. 'Anyone know him?'

The passengers shook their heads, one said 'no'. The driver shook out the stage-line manifest.

'His name was Hawkins,' he said, 'Nathan Hawkins of Las Noches.'

'Better get going in case they find their courage and come back,' said Bob.

'Should we bury the bodies, or take 'em into Prospect Falls?' asked the man tending to his wife.

'We'll load 'em into the boot of the coach and take 'em into the sheriff.' declared the driver.

When the bodies were loaded and secured Bob and Matt announced that they were headed for Prospect Falls and therefore would ride along with the coach.

Prospect Falls was a burgeoning town. It boasted two hotels, two saloons, a couple of cafés, two general-merchandise stores, a gunsmith, a blacksmith, a branch of the Cattleman's Bank, church, school, and a stage-line depot. It stood in the middle of a vast prairie thirty miles south of Fort Grainger. A tributary of the Rio Grande ran less than half a mile from the town boundary.

A weary Matt and Bob reined in outside the Carlton Hotel. They hitched the horses to the rail and stepped up on to the stoop, brushing white powdery dust from their clothes with their hats.

'I'll go get us a couple of rooms,' said Matt. He walked into the hotel, his high-heeled cowboy boots clomping on the wooden floorboards, accompanied by the musical jingling of his spurs. Although music didn't match Matt's sombre mood.

The bald-headed desk clerk set down his pen and looked up eagerly.

'Afternoon, sir. How can I help?' His even-toothed smile was very welcoming.

'I need two rooms for me and my partner. And we both could use a bath and a shave.'

'Front or back?' asked the clerk.

'What?'

'Rooms at the front or back of the hotel, which would you prefer? We have both available,' he added.

'Oh. Front then.'

'Excellent choice, sir,' said the clerk, reaching behind him to select two keys from brass hooks. 'If you will follow me.'

'No,' said Matt. 'You arrange the baths. We'll leave our possibles with you. Where's the livery?'

Once they had settled their horses at the livery stable, Matt and Bob strolled back to the Carlton Hotel. The obliging desk clerk showed them to their rooms; he had already taken up their belongings.

After a shave and a hot bath, and a couple of hours' rest, they commenced their search, starting with the hotel clerk and the other employees still on duty. Matt showed the small tintype of Joey, but after the encouraging news in Mesilla, the opposite was experienced in Prospect Falls. Everyone they asked shook their heads: not one person recognized the young man in the picture or would admit to having seen anyone like him.

It was the same at the other hotel and both of the town's saloons. The Eagle café was no different, although two cowboys looked a little sheepish as they denied any knowledge of Joey. Both men left hurriedly, before Matt had showed Joey's picture to each one of the diners. Their hasty departure would not normally have seemed surprising, except that neither man had totally finished his meal. For a cowboy to leave food was unusual. The waiter told Matt the cowboys both worked for the Bar C. *There it is again*, Matt said to himself, *everywhere we go we hear that name.*

Bob was waiting for Matt in the saloon bar of the hotel; he had no good news. No one he had spoken to had shown any signs of recognition. The only people not available had been the sheriff and his deputy, who were out of town, and the blacksmith and his wife, who were visiting relatives. They were expected back next morning. Matt announced that he was tired and was going to bed, leaving Bob to have another drink and a game of cards.

8

After he'd consumed a hearty Western breakfast Matt found Sheriff Wade in his office. He was a mature, big bear of a man, with greying hair and piercing flinty black eyes. His right cheek twitched when he spoke. He listened patiently to Matt's story before saying that he knew nothing of the youth.

'If he'd'a rode into my town, I would'a knowed about it,' he drawled. 'No, sir. The boy never reached Prospect Falls.' His right cheek twitched even more. There was something odd in Wade's manner that Matt couldn't put his finger on.

Matt shrugged off the feeling, shook the sheriff's hand and thanked him for his time, He needed to dry the sweat from his palm after releasing the lawman's hand.

Bob Crane met him in the street. 'Any luck?' he asked.

Matt shrugged. 'No. You?'

'No luck with the blacksmith. So I called in at the Eagle café again. Asked about them two cowpokes who left in a hurry last night. The owner confirmed that they work for the Bar C, owned by that feller named Henry John

Copeland. Folks around here call him H.J.' He gestured with a hand. 'I was just on the way to the livery to check on the horses.'

'I'll tag along.'

The ostler who had tended their horses the day before was rubbing down a big handsome palomino.

'Howdy fellers,' he greeted. 'Come to check on your horses?'

Matt nodded. 'Got a picture I'd appreciate you taking a look at.'

The ostler stopped what he was doing. 'A picture?'

'Yes. A tintype.' Matt fished the picture out of his shirt pocket and held it out.

The ostler wiped his hand on his apron and took it, alternately holding the picture close to his face, then at arm's length.

'Nope,' he said, 'sorry. Never set eyes on him. Well, not in person so to speak. Sorry,' he repeated.

'Thanks anyway,' said Matt. 'Is the owner in?'

The ostler nodded. 'He's in the office. Want me to get him for you?'

'No. We'll go see him.'

'OK. Well, nice meetin' you fellers. Your horses are in good shape. Let me know if there's anythin' else I can do for you.' The ostler went back to rubbing down the palomino.

Matt knocked politely on the office door.

'Come in,' a deep gruff voice called out.

The owner of the livery stable stood up behind his desk. A short man, barely five foot tall, wearing a white shirt and heavily creased black suit, his shiny hairless head reflected the sunlight that filtered through the large window at the side of his desk. He smiled a broad smile.

'Morning, gents. What can I do for you?'

Matt stuck out a hand. 'Name's Matt Walker.' He gestured to the big man at his shoulder, 'This is Bob Crane.'

The livery owner shook hands with both men. 'Captain Jack Connelly.' He grinned, 'Please take a seat.'

When Matt and Bob were seated Connelly asked, 'Coffee?'

'No thanks,' they chorused. Matt reached for the tintype.

'Would you look at this picture please? Tell me if you recognize the young man.'

Captain Connelly examined the tintype carefully. 'Nothin' shoots out at me,' he said, shaking his head. 'Don't guess I ever seen him. Couple of weeks ago, you said?'

Matt nodded.

'No. I've been away for nearly a month on my honeymoon,' Connelly said. 'Sorry,' he added handing back the picture. He leaned back in his chair and folded his arms. 'Anything else I can do for you?'

'No,' said Matt getting up from the chair. 'Obliged to you for looking. Thanks again. Oh, and congratulations on your marriage.'

'My pleasure. Just a shame I can't help you.'

The three men shook hands. Captain Connelly bade them goodbye and good luck. Matt and Bob decided to return to the hotel.

'Guess we've drawn another blank,' said Bob ruefully.

*

As soon as Matt Walker had left his office Sheriff Wade lost no time in deciding to ride out to see H.J. He called to a deputy to have his horse saddled.

Jez Moxley and three of the Bar C cowboys met him on the trail.

'Howdy, Jake,' said Moxley.

Sheriff Wade returned the ramrod's greeting.

'You headed for the Bar C?' asked Moxley.

Sheriff Wade nodded. 'I need to see H.J.'

'He ain't at home,' said one cowboy. 'Gone to Santa Fe on business.'

'When'll he be back?'

'Probably be gone for three or four days.' Moxley jumped in. 'Anythin' that won't keep?'

Sheriff Wade stroked his whiskered chin as he pondered what to say.

'Two fellers come into town yesterday.'

'So?' Moxley challenged.

'They were askin' if anybody had seen a young feller. Had one of them tintype pictures.'

'So, who's gone missin'?'

'Joseph Crane.'

Moxley started at hearing the name, his eyes widened questioningly, but before he could say anything the sheriff added, 'Yep. You know the one.'

Moxley leaned back in his saddle. Leather creaked as he took off his stained Stetson. He wiped the sweat from his brow with a sleeve, his face momentarily blank, searching for a question.

'Who was it was askin'?'

Sheriff Wade tipped his hat back. 'One was a feller

named Walker. Matt Walker. Name mean anythin' to you?'
Moxley shook his head.

Sheriff Wade continued, 'The other feller's name's Bob
Crane. Buckskins, long hair. Got the look of an Indian
fighter.'

'Bob Crane, you say?' Moxley queried. Wade nodded.
Moxley's gravelly voice took on a more aggressive tone.

'Any relation to the kid?'

'Didn't say, but I reckon they must be.'

'They look like they could handle themselves?'

'Yep. Walker's Colt was tied down, gunslinger style. The
grip looked like it had seen plenty of action.'

'Hmm,' pondered Moxley.

'What's H.J. doing in Santa Fe?'

Moxley shrugged. 'Didn't say.'

'Didn't you ask him?'

'No.'

Wade sniffed, recognizing a fruitless conversation when
he heard one.

'OK, I'll get back to town. Make sure nobody talks.
Send me word when H.J. gets back.'

'Will do,' Moxley promised.

In the first-floor front room of the hotel Matt Walker
moved the flimsy lace curtain to one side so he could see
down the street. The welcome breeze that wafted over his
face brought some relief from the heat of the morning.
He was tired – the search for Joey had taken its toll on his
body as well as his spirit; he hadn't expected the quest to
go on so long. And now he was beginning to fear the
worst.

He was sure the key to finding out about Joey's disappearance was to be found in Prospect Falls; nothing he had seen or heard so far would change this. Matt couldn't put his finger on exactly what it was that convinced him that he was right; it was a whole bunch of things – feelings, sixth sense, call it what you like, but whatever it was, it was there. Like the way some people averted their eyes when he showed them Joey's picture; the way those cowboys upped and left their meals. Lots of tiny things.

Below the window a dog barked loudly, snapping Matt from his thoughts and startling a pair of horses pulling a heavily laden open-backed wagon along the almost deserted street. The driver shouted and struggled long and hard to regain control of the team as, panicked by the dog, both horses reared and snorted. A couple of nosy citizens stood watching the entertainment, then, once the fun was over, resumed their passage along the sidewalk.

Directly across from the hotel a group of four or five children were playing at the head of an alleyway. Matt wondered why they were not in school, then tried to figure out what day this was. He decided it must be Saturday.

Two well-armed cowboys rode past, oblivious of the man watching them from the hotel window. An ancient looking Mexican peon clad in a dirty white shirt and trousers pulled hard on a rope attached to a stubborn moth-eaten donkey, all the time glancing nervously around; maybe Prospect Falls was not a friendly place for Mexicans. The noisy dog had disappeared. Matt was shaken from his thoughts by a loud knock on the door.

Leaving the window and the interesting view of the street, he moved across the room.

'Yes?' he called out.

'It's me. Bob!'

Matt turned the over-elaborate key in the lock and opened the door. Bob Crane looked smart in clean shirt and denims. He twirled his hat on one forefinger as he stepped across the threshold. Matt noticed Bob's hair – it was plastered down with hair oil, the centre parting looked like it had been made with a razor and straight-edge.

'You smell pretty,' said Matt, sniffing the air. 'Meeting anybody special?'

Bob grinned wryly. 'Show some respect for your elders,' he warned, wagging a finger. 'Just paid a visit to the barber's, that's all.'

'Oh.' Matt chuckled, as if it wasn't obvious.

'Let's go get something to eat before you die of laughing,' suggested Bob.

Matt picked up his hat from the bed and buckled on his gun-belt. 'OK, let's go, *amigo*,' he said.

The desk clerk pointed them toward the Sunburst café.

'Best eats in town,' he recommended. 'Eat there meself.'

9

The café was only about half-full, the smells were delicious. An impressively neat and tidy sort of place with pretty red-and-white chequered tablecloths, and white-painted walls. A tubby, elderly, bald man with a foreign accent, a droopy grey moustache, and slightly stained white apron tied around his amble girth ushered them to a table. Other diners smiled a friendly greeting as Matt and Bob passed by.

'Seems a homely place,' Bob commented as they took a seat. 'Clean, not like the Eagle café.' He picked up a fork. 'Nice,' he said.

'What can I get you gents?' the waiter enquired.

Matt answered first. 'I'll have a big steak. Bloody, couple of fried eggs on top, and some fried potatoes,' he stated. 'I'm starving. Ravenous,' he added for good measure.

'I'll have the same,' said Bob.

'Coffee?'

Matt looked at Bob, who nodded.

'Yes thanks,' he said, 'and a pitcher of cold water.'

The waiter scurried away, returning twice during the

following moments with cups and saucers, a pot of coffee, water and a couple of glasses.

A dusty cowboy came in to loud greetings from two others seated at a table in the window. His footfall, and the metallic jingle of his big Texas spurs sounded loud in the momentary silence. The range rider slapped the cowboy nearest to him on the back and sat down, unbuckling his spurs and setting them on the vacant chair next to him. The sound of their happy conversation filled the room, punctuated by bursts of loud guffaws and hearty laughter.

'Somebody's happy,' Matt observed, tilting his head to one side; the sounds reminded him of time spent in the company of good, honest, hard-working cowhands. He wasn't able to hear what the cowboys were saying, but guessed it was the usual joshing and friendly insults.

The food arrived and they tucked in heartily. The waiter reappeared.

'Everything OK, gents?' he enquired genuinely.

Matt and Bob nodded out a chorused, 'Good. Thanks.'

The steaks were excellent, tasty and cooked perfectly.

'Hans!' The diminutive waiter turned to face the female voice. All heads in the room turned in unison. Standing in the open doorway was an extremely handsome red-haired woman.

'I need a hand in the kitchen.' She flashed an even-toothed all-encompassing smile at the diners, and raised a slender hand to one of the cowboys. He then stood and called out,

'Hey, Amelia. When you gonna say yes, and make me a happy man?' He pressed his left hand across his heart as he asked the question.

Her smile broadened, her emerald-green eyes flashed, 'Maybe one day, Vince.' She laughed as she turned on her heel. The little waiter followed her into the kitchen.

'Ain't she somethin'?' Matt heard the cowboy named Vince say.

'Close your mouth,' Bob told Matt.

'What?'

'I said, close your mouth. Before your teeth fall out.'

Matt grinned. 'Well, you have to admit she is one good-looking woman.'

'Can't argue with that,' Bob agreed.

The waiter appeared. 'Piece of pie to finish?' he asked, clearing away the dishes.

'Maybe later,' said Bob. 'Give us a few minutes.'

'More coffee, then?'

'OK,' said Matt. 'Who was that?' He couldn't help himself. He had to know who she was.

'Who?' asked the waiter, 'Oh, the lady?' he said, finally understanding Matt's question. 'That's Mrs Healey,' he said. 'She owns the Sunburst café.'

'And the cowboys?' Matt motioned his head towards the table in the window.

'Bar C riders,' the waiter answered. 'Nice bunch. Always leave a good tip,' he added suggestively. 'Ready for that pie? It's apple. Very good.'

'I'll take a slice,' said Bob, feeling his mouth begin to water.

Matt held up a hand. 'Nothing for me, thanks.'

The three cowboys got up and left noisily, amidst another round of guffaws and back-slapping. The one named Vince patted the waiter's head as he made for the door.

All but one of the other diners had already left. The last one departed as Bob was finishing his piece of apple pie.

The waiter returned right on cue. 'Tasty?' he enquired.

Bob agreed. 'Enjoyed every mouthful,' he said, taking out the makings. He rolled a smoke, lit it, drew in a deep lungful, then coughed.

'Why don't you stop smoking those things?' said Matt. 'Smells like old leaves.'

'Should do,' replied Bob. 'That's what they are, but don't taste as bad as some I've smoked.' He grinned. 'You never smoked?' he asked.

'Never saw the need,' said Matt. 'Seems to me you'd get the same effect from standing close to a fire.'

Matt took out the tintype. 'Ever see this young man?' he asked the waiter.

The little man took the picture and examined it carefully. He shook his head.

'No. Sorry. I do not recognize him. I do not believe I have ever seen him. Nice-looking boy,' he added. 'What has he done?'

'Nothing,' replied Matt. 'We are just looking for him. Wondered if you recalled seeing him.'

The waiter realized there was more to the story he was being told, but decided against enquiring further.

'Mind if I ask Mrs Healey?' Matt asked politely.

'Er . . . no.' The waiter was puzzled as to why the man had bothered to ask.

Matt pushed back the chair and walked over to the kitchen door. He knocked. A smooth velvety voice answered softly. 'Yes?'

The door opened fully, and Matt was face to face with the most beautiful woman he had ever seen in his life. Her forehead was beaded with perspiration. She brushed a loose strand of red hair from her brow and tucked it behind one ear. For a moment, faced with such an attractive woman, Matt found he was tongue-tied.

Her smooth flawless skin was the colour of ivory, emphasizing the flaming red of her hair, worn pinned up in a large bun at the back of her head. He put her age at close to his: at around thirty-five. Her full red mouth smiled questioningly at him.

'Something wrong with the food?' She asked.

'N . . . no!' Matt blushed, backing away. She stepped into the dining room. 'I wanted to ask you to take a look at this picture.' He held the tintype out to her. She took it from him.

'Step over to the window, it's lighter there. I'll see better.' Mrs Healey shook her head gently from side to side. 'I really am sorry, but I'm afraid I don't recognize him.' She looked into Matt's eyes. 'Who is he?' she asked.

'His name is Joseph Crane, we call him Joey. He is nineteen years old, going on fifty. Me and that big fellow over there are two of his uncles.'

She looked across to where Bob was sitting, drinking a cup of coffee, and smiled a greeting. Bob raised a hand.

'Joey's missing,' Matt added. 'We're trying to figure out where he's got to. He was supposed to be visiting me in Arizona. Should have arrived weeks ago.' Matt hadn't intended to tell her or anyone else the full story, but he hadn't been able to stop himself. Mrs Healey seemed to be one of those people who instinctively gain your trust the moment you meet them.

'I'm sorry I'm not able to help.' Her soothing words broke the temporary silence that had descended.

Matt glanced at Bob, shaking his head. He turned back to the woman. 'Name's Matt Walker, ma'am.'

'Amelia Healey,' she announced, taking Matt's hand.

Her skin was warm, and smooth as cream. Matt didn't want to let go.

She pulled away. 'Well . . . if everything was OK. I really must get on.'

'Yes. Of course,' Matt apologized, adding, 'The meal was great.'

'Good.' She smiled. 'I'm glad you enjoyed it. Call again, won't you? Tonight's special is slow-cooked beef stew and dumplings.' She turned to go back to the kitchen.

Matt's eyes took in the gentle sway of her hips as she walked away; she seemed to glide noiselessly across the floor. He shook his head gently, his thoughts filled with the memory of her loveliness. He felt Bob's powerful grip on his arm.

'Come on. We got work to do,' said Bob.

10

'Amelia!' Copeland shouted. Amelia Healey's head popped round the open kitchen door.

'What?' she called back.

'That was one heck of a meal.' Copeland said in a much softer voice. 'Just wanted to tell you what a great cook you are.'

'Thanks,' she acknowledged. Copeland pushed back his chair with a scrape and turned to face her.

'When are you going to hand in your apron and come live at the Bar C?'

She leaned a hand on the white-painted doorframe and eyed the rancher with a fixed stare.

'Never,' she said, disappearing into the kitchen, slamming the door shut behind her.

Amelia Healey had never quite figured out how she felt about H.J. Copeland. She knew his reputation as a hard man to deal with – word was that nobody got the better of the rancher. But despite this surface harshness, on occasions she had witnessed some of his better side. Like the fact that he always removed his hat when speaking to a female, always stood when a woman came into a room. There were those who thought his politeness was an act, a mask to hide his true nature; she wasn't one of those people. On the other hand, she reflected, a man doesn't get to be the biggest rancher in the territory and head of a successful copper-mining business without having a ruthless streak.

Her thoughts strayed to a time not long after H.J's divorce when she had warmed to him. He had showered her with gifts and a great deal of his attention. She had been flattered that this wealthy man, who could surely have his pick of women, had singled her out to be the object of his affection. He wasn't bad looking, but it was his confident air that was most attractive.

The son of an Englishman who had made it big in the gold fields, and the young daughter of Irish immigrants, Henry John Copeland had grown up in a wealthy household. He had been educated expensively in Boston before travelling the world in style. Experienced in finance, he had taken over a small ranch purchased years earlier by his father, which H.J. had built into a huge cattle empire, founding the town of Prospect Falls in the process.

She had no romantic feelings for the man, but life as the consort of a rich man did bring its own appeal to a woman who had worked hard all her life. A woman who recognized the power she held over men, Amelia Healey worked hard at maintaining the good looks that nature had bestowed upon her. A smooth and flawless alabaster complexion, eyes that sparkled, hair that shone like the sun, and a radiant personality, rounded off a shapely figure of near-perfect proportions. She smiled to herself as she caught her reflection in the long mirror that hung on one wall of the kitchen.

Back in the café, H. J. Copeland tried to laugh off her crushing reply, but in reality the rejection hurt him deeply: he wasn't used to not getting his way. Amelia Healey had sought to embarrass him many times; one day she would do it once too often. His cheeks glowed blood-red as he let out a loud guffaw aimed at fooling anyone brave enough to cast a judgemental eye in his direction, or say or do anything that would increase the embarrassment he was feeling. He smiled a false smile at a couple of the other diners, but inside he was seething. But before he could say or do anything to retrieve his self-respect the café door burst open. One of the Bar C ranch hands rushed over to Copeland's table.

'Boss. Boss.' the cowhand yelled. Copeland looked round at the ruddy-faced cowhand. 'There's trou—' the cowboy suddenly realized that in his excitement he was speaking too loud. He paused, bending his head towards his boss.

'There's trouble, boss,' he whispered. 'Jez sent me to get you.'

Copeland glared into the cowboy's flushed face, his eyes demanding more information.

'He's caught another rustler.'

Copeland was on his feet in a flash. Grabbing his hat from the hatstand he followed the cowboy out into the street. The ostler from the livery stable was holding Copeland's palomino.

'I sent someone to get your horse, boss. Figured you'd want to be away fast.'

'Good thinking,' Copeland said, mounting the big palomino. 'Lead on.'

A cloud of dust rose from the horses' hoofs as employer and employee raced away.

Her attention drawn by the commotion, Amelia Healey leaned one shoulder against the open doorway.

'What do you suppose that was all about?' she wondered.

Hans, her little German waiter, moved a couple of steps closer to her, and answered her question.

'The cowhand who came in said there was trouble on Bar C range,' His voice became hushed. 'Jez Moxley's caught another rustler.'

Amelia folded her arms. 'Go tell the sheriff,' she ordered.

The waiter removed his apron and went off to do his employer's bidding. On the way Hans encountered a number of citizens who enquired as to the reason for his haste, and in less than ten minutes the story was all around town, suitably embellished with gory details concocted in the little German's imagination.

Sheriff Wade shouted to a deputy to get his horse as Hans left his office. Then, mounted, he headed out of town at top speed.

H.J. Copeland looked down at the hog-tied figure. He addressed his foreman.

'Who is he?'

Jez Moxley tipped back his black Stetson with a finger. 'Says his name is Pierre Lamont, from New Orleans. Swears he's a gambler by trade.' Moxley grabbed the trussed-up man by the collar of his black drape coat and hauled him to his feet.

'I *am* Pierre Lamont,' the man pleaded in a shaky voice, his French accent heavy and obvious.

Copeland could see from the cut on the man's lip and the bruises on his face that Moxley had already given him a good going over.

'I have not done anything.' He was scared, his eyes wild with fear. 'If I have inadvertently strayed on to your land, Monsieur, I am sorry. I. . . .' His attempted explanation was cut short by the force of Moxley's fist. Blood spurted from the man's lip and nose as he flew backwards to land in a heap. He was out cold.

H.J. Copeland eyed his foreman with more than a little suspicion.

'Evidence?' he said simply. Moxley flung out an arm.

'Take a look in that gunny sack hanging from his saddle pommel.'

Copeland held a hand out. One of his cowhands lifted the sack from the stranger's horse and handed it to his boss.

Copeland lifted out two brown-paper packages and unwrapped each in turn; both contained a hunk of bloody meat.

'The steer he cut that off is hidden in the brush about half a mile east of here,' said Moxley.

H.J. Copeland pushed the meat back into the sack, and tossed the sack to the cowboy. He wasn't exactly suspicious, but he was wary.

Moxley saw how his boss had reacted, and added: 'I recognized him as soon as I saw him, boss. He's one of the rustlers I chased last week. The one that took a shot at me. Remember? I told you about it. I'd recognize that black rig of his anywhere.'

Copeland stroked his chin. 'You're sure?'

Moxley didn't hesitate. 'Certain sure, boss.'

H.J. Copeland took out a leather cigar case from the inside pocket of his coat and selected a cigar. He bit off the end and spat out the plug. A match flared. Copeland lit up.

'Want me to see to it?' asked Moxley.

Copeland sucked in a lungful of cigar smoke and pondered for a moment. He nodded, coming to a decision.

'See to it.' He turned away, deciding not to stick around for the main event. He slipped an expensively booted foot into the stirrup and mounted his horse.

At that moment Sheriff Wade galloped up, reining in his mount in a cloud of dust. His keen eyes took in the scene in one look.

'What's happening?'

Moxley took it upon himself to answer. 'Another rustler,' he said. 'No need for you to get involved. I got it all under control.' He grinned. 'We can handle what needs doing.' The sheriff ignored him and spoke to H.J. Copeland.

'H.J., can I have a word with you?' he asked politely, though there was an edge to his voice.

'Speak up,' Copeland urged the lawman.

'In private,' said Wade. 'I need to speak to you in private,' he emphasized.

Copeland motioned to the sheriff to follow him. He urged his horse into a walk, halting in a small stand of cottonwoods fifteen or twenty yards from where his men stood watching. Wade followed.

Copeland turned, saddle leather creaking loudly. 'Well?' he demanded, not happy with the sheriff's arrival.

Wade looked nervously at the rancher, hating to be the one to caution Copeland.

'H.J.,' he said, 'please don't let this happen.'

'Let what happen?'

'What Moxley's doing is wrong, and you know it.' Copeland looked impassively at the sheriff, but said nothing. 'It's getting more and more difficult to keep a lid on it. People are starting to talk.'

'Let them.'

'I don't like it, H.J. I'm hearing too many rumours.' Wade glanced at the rancher. Copeland was scowling at him. 'One more might be one too many.' He felt Copeland's eyes bore into him as though the rancher were looking inside his head.

Undeterred, the sheriff carried on: 'I'm only looking out for your interests, H.J.,' he said. 'There's rumours we might get a visit from US marshals.'

Copeland ground his teeth together. 'Wade,' he said, 'you're losing your nerve. Haven't I always looked after you? Haven't I always seen to it that you've been well compensated for your service? Do I need to get me another sheriff?' No one could mistake the rancher's chilling words for anything less than a threat.

'N . . . No!' Sheriff Wade protested. 'I'm just warning . . .' he stopped abruptly in mid-sentence, knowing he had chosen the wrong word.

'Warning?' Copeland barked out. '*You* are warning *me?*'

The sheriff wished a hole would open up for him to hide in.

'No, H.J.,' he protested. 'You got it all wrong. I was warning you of a potential problem.'

'You best get back to town in case some drunks need locking up.' The rancher's tone was sarcastic. 'Go on, now.'

Sheriff Wade realized how much he hated H.J. Copeland. At that moment he could have willingly taken out his pistol and shot him, but he knew such a thing wasn't an option. He'd lived high on the hog since he'd become one of Copeland's paid men. He raised a hand in farewell, and rode away, tail between his legs. As he rode he remembered back to a time when he would not have allowed any man to speak so to him. Whatever doubts he had, he'd always believed in keeping them to himself. Men respected confidence – took readily to orders from a man who was sure of himself. Today had not been the day to change this philosophy.

H.J. Copeland's horse knew the way home as well as its master. The horse pulled up outside the sprawling ranch house jarring Copeland from his thoughts. The rancher snapped back to reality with a jolt. He looked around vacantly, for a moment not realizing he had arrived home. He didn't remember much, if anything, of the ride back to the Bar C, so deep in thought had he been.

He hadn't waited to witness the stringing up of the latest rustler Moxley had caught. Just as he hadn't waited to watch the lynching of the previous victim of Moxley's version of range justice. Copeland knew full well that the ultimate responsibility lay with him. A strong word from him would have brought any lynching to a halt well before the offender had died. In truth, he had had enough of this senseless killing, and he was heartily sick of the cattle business. And even more so, he was sick of his life.

What was really going on? Neither of Moxley's two previous victims, whom the ramrod had insisted were part of the gang of cattle-thieves had looked anything like he expected cattle rustlers to look. And the remaining question was why, when so many of these so-called rustlers had been caught and hanged, had the rustling of Bar C cattle actually increased?

'Why?' Copeland said out loud. It just didn't stack up.

The gunmen he had sent for came highly recommended. Other prominent cattlemen in the state cattleman's association had used the Stanton brothers successfully in the recent past. Copeland was relying on them to resolve all his problems; maybe then he would have a chance of finding the peace he desired.

The two Stanton brothers, Joe and Mike, had gained a reputation as deadly, cold-bloodied killers who fixed unfixable problems. They didn't come cheap, but the way things were going he couldn't afford not to pay their exorbitant fee. They had wired him to advise acceptance of his offer of their rates and terms and when to expect them to arrive in Prospect Falls. It was all very businesslike.

11

The two men stood ten feet apart.

'Tex said you were lookin' fer me?' Moxley challenged frostily.

He'd been drinking. Sheriff Wade could smell whiskey on him. Suddenly, faced by the big foreman, Wade's courage began to evaporate fast. He was beginning to wish he hadn't put the word out.

Word had come to him from an old friend in the governor's office in Santa Fe that complaints about H.J. Copeland and the way the Bar C operated were going to be investigated. Wade knew that the time had come for him to be seen to act like a real lawman. His idea, coming to him as he lay in bed the night before, was that if he could arrest Moxley he would thereby demonstrate to all that he was his own man, and not in league with the Bar C.

Sheriff Wade eyed his opponent cautiously. In the old days, when he had been a much younger man, he wouldn't have shown one moment's hesitation. By now he would be blowing gunsmoke away from the end of his Colt

Peacemaker, a man lying on the ground, dead at his feet. Wade smiled inwardly at the memory of days long since past when he had been lightning-fast. Not just fast, but a level or two above real fast. It was that confident dead-eyed speed that had brought him a mean reputation. A reputation men feared, one that had enabled him to live high on the hog for years. Now, he knew, that speed had deserted him: dissipated by years of drink and general overindulgence.

'Well? What's it to be, Sheriff?' Moxley's voice was harsh and cold.

Wade's attention snapped back to the present; his mouth was suddenly as dry as the underside of a desert snake's belly. He inched his right hand away from his six-gun and hooked a thumb on to his gunbelt. He relaxed his muscles, trying hard to keep his face from twitching.

'Don't get riled, Jez. I didn't mean nothin'.' Wade hated the cringing cowardice in his voice.

Moxley didn't relax one iota. He moved forward, and poked a finger into the sheriff's chest.

'Wade. You better be more careful what you say if you don't feel you can back it up.' Moxley turned away, unable and unwilling to hide the sneer of contempt on his face.

In contrast Sheriff Wade stared straight ahead, knowing that his cowardice was out there in the open for all to see. His hands trembled uncontrollably, the flush of embarrassment and shame coursed through his entire body. It was some moments before he could move, and even then his knees were like jelly and his mouth seemed to be crammed with cotton.

He shuddered as he watched Moxley enter the Golden

Nugget saloon in the full knowledge that his backbone had all but disappeared. It wasn't a cold day but he couldn't stop his body from shivering.

H.J. Copeland thought back. Had it really been over five years since his second wife had left him? The acrimonious divorce had gone through two years earlier on the grounds of his continued adultery. Jane Copeland hadn't taken her husband to her bed for more years than H.J. wanted to recall. It was a mystery to him why he had ever agreed to marry the woman. Yes, she had breeding, as the daughter of an established banking family, but as a wife she had left a lot to be desired. She had been as barren as a desert when it came to giving him an heir. A woman repressed sexually, she had shown distaste for even the slightest show of affection, hated the sex act, rebutting his needs at every turn, offering one feeble excuse after another.

The only sound in the room came from a constant buzzing of flies.

The couple's differences regarding sex were unresolvable, but Copeland had resigned himself to the situation, choosing to take his favours to the kind of women who had no scruples in accepting his generous payments of money and gifts.

Life with Jane had become tolerable until one fateful day. He had never found out the specific details behind Jane's change. All he knew was that her hatred of his foreman, Jez Moxley, escalated dramatically. She would never say what had so alienated her from the big ramrod. One day everything was OK; next day she had packed her belongings and left.

The divorce had been a bad-tempered and long-drawn-out affair, despite the generous settlement H.J. had agreed to. It hadn't been a difficult decision: he could afford it.

Now, out of the blue, she had written to him, asking for more money. Asking him to come to New York to see her. He had no intention of handing over any more of his fortune, and even less of a notion to go anywhere near the she-cat. Involuntarily his hand went to his cheek where, on close inspection, the scars caused by her fingernails were still visible. As far as he could recall, during that attack she had been more aroused than he had ever seen her.

Just lately Copeland found himself increasingly pondering his life and how a lot of things had got out of hand. This business about rustlers and lynching ate away at his sensibility. He couldn't recall how it had all started, but knew in his heart that taking the law into his own hands was in itself against the law.

It had been different in the old days. Then it was dog eat dog. There had been no law around in those early days: a man had to protect what was his by any means possible, and if that meant taking a life, then so be it. Henry John Copeland didn't want to be outside the law: he wanted to be inside it. But how should he go about the task of being recognized as a law-abiding citizen? He had the wealth to make himself anything he wanted to be. Heck, he could even be governor one day.

He thought about his vast wealth, and how immensely rich he was in material things. But despite lacking for nothing on that score there were in other respects gaping holes in his life: for all his money and possessions he had no real friends. He was unhappy in the extreme.

H.J. needed women. His voracious sexual appetite had diminished not one iota with the passing years. Three young Mexican women lived on the Bar C in a sturdily built log cabin that he had built specially for them some fifty or so yards from the main house. A covered walkway linked the two buildings. He had never seen any of the women as anything more than a vessel for his carnal cravings.

Two days later, H.J. Copeland walked into Drummond's Hotel in Prospect Falls. He stopped in front of the desk.

'Mr Stanton's room number, please. Joe Stanton,' he added.

'Mr Stanton and his brother are in the saloon bar, Mr Copeland,' the clerk informed him.

Despite it not yet being noon there were five or six people in the hotel bar enjoying a pre-lunchtime drink. Two men stood out from the rest.

The Stanton brothers sat at a table against the far wall of the bar from where they had an excellent view of both entrances. Outwardly they looked like a couple of successful businessmen. Clean shaven, both wore expensive black suits, white shirts and black neckties. Black narrow-brimmed, flat-crowned hats hid their eyes. In the centre of the table in front of them were three white china cups and saucers and a large pot of coffee. All seemed safe and serene until one noticed the twelve-gauge shotguns leaning against the side of each of the chairs the brothers were sitting upon.

H.J. Copeland stood in the doorway for a couple of

seconds, looking around the bar room. The man to the left of the group lifted his right leg to place the sole of his highly polished boot on the seat of a spare chair, which he pushed away from the table.

'Chair,' he said. It was an order, not a question. His half-whispered voice sounded gravelly-harsh. His accent was Eastern, educated, cultured.

Copeland couldn't make up his mind which or all of the words were the most appropriate description. He allowed the batwing doors to slip from his grasp, to close behind him with a noisy clatter. He walked over to the table in a slow lope, designed to give the impression that he was cool and confident. The chair creaked loudly when he sat down.

'Coffee?' Joe Stanton lifted the coffee pot and poured out a fresh cup without waiting for Copeland's answer.

The rancher noticed the man's thick, strong wrist. He raised the china cup to his lips and took a sip. The coffee was hot and bitter.

'I'm Joe, this is Mike,' Stanton said abruptly, not holding out his hand.

Copeland nodded a terse greeting to both men.

'Well?' Joe Stanton frowned. 'You sent for us.' He paused to look at his brother, then turned back. 'Brought the money?'

'Yes.' Copeland looked around furtively, then drew a thick brown envelope from his inside coat pocket and handed it over.

Joe Stanton took the envelope and without checking the contents passed it to his brother.

Copeland coughed nervously. 'When can. . . ?' He

checked himself mid-question and rephrased it. 'When do you anticipate being able to start?'

Joe glanced at his brother, who shot a broad grin back in his direction.

'We started at first light,' he said icily.

There was menace in Stanton's tone, which only served to enhance the visual impression Copeland had already formed. The Stanton brothers looked every bit as mean and ruthless as their reputation. H.J. was happy with his choice.

12

Outside the general store Bob turned to Matt.

'I need some tobacco. You carry on, I'll catch up.'

'It's OK, I'll come with you.'

The air inside the store was cool. Aromas of molasses and leather pervaded the dust-filled air. Bob strode purposefully up to the counter. Matt wandered around tables filled with jars, tins, and bolts of cloth.

'Howdy, gents.' A tall thin man in a long white apron stuck out a hand. 'Baylis Harding's the name, like the sign says. Folks call me Bay.' He had the genuine smile of an easy-going man.

'Thought it was the name of a partnership,' said Bob.

'No.' Harding chuckled, 'Lots of folks do. Confusing I guess.'

Bob nodded. 'Baylis is an unusual Christian name.'

'Yes it is, ain't it? Family tradition. Come over from England, so my ma always told me. Listen to me prattle on. Wife's always telling me to quit jawing so much. Anyway, what can I do for you?'

'Tobacco,' Bob answered.

'I'll show you what we've got.' The storekeeper turned and grabbed several brands. He spread them out on the counter. 'Take your pick.' He grinned.

Towards the back of the store Matt's eye was drawn to a fine-looking saddle. He moved across the wooden floor and examined it closely.

'Hey, mister,' he called out. Baylis Harding turned to look at Matt. 'This is a fine-looking saddle.'

'Sure is.' Harding nodded. 'Finest leather.'

'Is it for sale?'

'Yes, of course.'

'Looks used.'

'Yes, but not much. Still looks new,' Harding suggested. 'I can do you a real good price if you're interested.'

'Where'd you get it?'

Harding screwed up his face in concentration. 'Oh.' He looked perplexed. 'I dunno. Got it from some drifter passing through, I guess. You want to buy it?'

Matt shook his head. 'No. Just wondered.'

Bob selected the brand of tobacco he preferred, together with some cigarette papers, and paid the store-keeper.

'Call again,' Baylis Harding said as they walked out of the store.

Outside, Bob asked, 'What was with the interest in the saddle?'

'I recognized it. It's Joey's.'

'How do you know?'

'I gave it to him for his eighteenth birthday, just after his pa died. His initials are under the skirt, burned in. Had it done myself.'

Sleeves rolled up, shirt half-open, Matt Walker sat on a chair opposite the open window of his hotel room, gloomily staring at the tin-type of his nephew he held in one hand. Taken a few years earlier, the image of Joey smiled up at him. Matt swatted away an annoying fly and shook away the tears threatening to form. He didn't want to accept the negative but logical thoughts about the likelihood of finding Joey alive. For some time he had guessed that the youngster was dead, although he had fought shy of allowing himself to form that definitive word, constantly telling himself that he must remain hopeful.

The room was unbelievably hot, raising his level of intolerance. The fly that moments ago had been crawling along happily on the small table at his elbow now lay squashed under the force of Matt's left hand. He brushed the cadaver away, not wanting to accept the inevitability of a bad ending to the quest he and Bob had pledged themselves to, but suspecting the futility of retaining hope. Thus far every bit of information gleaned so diligently indicated the worst outcome. Matt felt sure that his fears coincided with those of Bob, although neither had voiced as much to the other.

A loud crack of thunder shook him from his melancholy mood. He got up from the chair and crossed to the open sash window, just managing to pull down the top section a second or two before the deluge hit the building. Big spots of rain banged down on the roof of the hotel, setting up a rhythmical beat reminiscent of a thousand drummers. Outside the cloud-crammed sky was almost pitch black, as though night-time had come early to Prospect Falls instead of it being just after noon.

As if mesmerized Matt watched the rain stream down the windowpane. Then, just as suddenly as it had started, the rain stopped.

Minutes later the sound of many hoofs echoed from building to building. Drawn to the sound, Matt moved to the window, pulled it open and looked out. Leading a column of *vaqueros* up the main street of Prospect Falls was Hector Cervantes, his high-stepping palomino a handsome sight to see. Hector reined in outside the hotel and stepped gracefully down from his mount. He saw Matt leaning out of the window and raised a hand in greeting.

'Matt,' he called out, 'I have something interesting to show you.'

'Be right down,' Matt called back. He buckled on his gunbelt and grabbed his hat.

Bob Crane was already halfway down the wide sweeping staircase by the time Matt reached the landing. Bob waited for Matt to catch up, then they descended to the lobby together. Hector stood in the doorway.

'What is it?' asked Matt.

'Outside,' Hector said sombrely. He led the way into the street. Several of the *vaqueros* tipped their sombreros, and urged their horses aside. In the centre of the group of riders stood a big sorrel with three white stockings. The body of a dead cowboy was draped across the horse's back.

Hector pointed. 'See the brand?' he said. 'CC. Your nephew's brand, *si*?'

'*Sí*,' Matt answered. He stepped closer to the horse to examine the brand, Bob Crane at his shoulder.

Bob ran a finger across the unmistakable indentation in the animal's coat.

'That's Joey's horse,' he exclaimed, 'no doubt about it.'

Hector anticipated the next question. 'This cowboy was discovered near the northern boundary of my land, where it abuts on the Bar C. He was dead – shot. The horse was near by. It must have run away.'

Matt pointed to the corpse. 'Know who he is?'

'No. But Luiz believes he is one of the Bar C riders. Or,' he added, 'I should say, was. I have sent Luiz to fetch the sheriff. I am certain he will know the cowboy's identity.'

An out-of-breath bartender arrived a few minutes later, trailing after Hector's *segundo*.

'Nobody in the sheriff's office,' said Luiz.

The bartender jerked the dead cowboy's head up by the hair, and examined the face closely.

'Blackie. Jim Black,' he corrected. 'Worked for the Bar C till a couple of weeks ago.' He looked at the big sorrel. 'But that's not his horse. He always rode a buckskin.' He let go the cowboy's hair, and the lifeless head banged against the horse's flank. The bartender shot a glance sideways. 'Has Sheriff Wade seen this?'

'Not as yet.' replied Hector.

'I'd better go get him then.' The bartender shot off at top speed. He returned moments later with one of Sheriff Wade's deputies.

'Sheriff's out of town,' the deputy told them. 'Let's take a look.' He lifted the cowboy's head up as the bartender had done. 'Yep,' he licked his lips as though savouring a tasty morsel of food, 'that's Blackie all right. No doubt about it.'

Matt slapped his hand against his leg. 'That does it.' He grimaced. 'First we find Joey's saddle, now his horse. Somebody around here is trying to give us the run-around.'

'You ain't kidding,' agreed Bob.

13

'Hey! Young feller!'

Matt turned sharply. The owner of the livery stable was jogging after him waving one hand in the air.

Matt stopped and waited for him to catch up. 'Captain Connelly. How are you, sir?'

'Well, thank you. I was thinking about what you were asking last time we met, and I remembered that I had employed a night guard to look after the stable while I and my new bride were away. Harve Stoltz. That's his name. Might be worth checking with him.'

'Where does he live?'

'He owns a small farm about fifteen miles west of town.'

'Thanks.'

Matt found Bob, and the pair of them rode off to Harve Stoltz's farm.

Harve was a big bluff man with an over-long, unkempt beard and moustache. He toted a shotgun menacingly until Matt told him why they were there.

'Yes. Oh no!' He dropped the shotgun and his hands flew to his mouth when he realized what he was about to

101

tell. 'I am so very sorry. You say he was your nephew?'

'Was?'

'What?'

'You said, *he was your nephew?*'

'Sorry. I don't like to have to tell you this, but there ain't no easy way to say it. Your nephew is dead.'

The news hit the two brothers-in-law hard; despite maintaining a positive attitude both had feared the worst. Bob was first to collect himself. He bit back the pain.

'Please tell us what you know,' he asked.

'Come up on to the porch and sit a spell.'

When Bob and Matt had sat down Harve told them what had happened.

'I was making my rounds of the stable yard before bedding down for the night, when three vagrants brought in a body draped across the back of a mule. They told me where they had found it, and showed me the paper that was pinned to the young man's chest when they found him.' Harve didn't want to say the word lynched, and tried hard to avoid giving too much detail.

'What did the paper say?'

'A name was written in capital letters.'

Both Bob and Matt knew the answer before Matt asked: 'What was the name?'

Harve hesitated for a second or two. 'Joseph Crane,' he said eventually. 'I am so sorry.'

Bob wrapped his fingers around Matt's arm for support.

'How was he killed?' Matt asked in a shaky voice.

'They said there was a rope around his neck.' Harve was reluctant to say more.

Tears were forming in Matt's eyes. 'So somebody had

lynched him?' he asked.

Harve looked down at the ground and nodded.

The news of Joey's death didn't come as a complete shock, but learning that their nephew had been lynched cut right to their hearts. Both fought back the tears. Thoughts of revenge tingled through their veins.

'What happened to his body?'

Harve Stoltz ignored Matt's question and decided to tell more of what he knew. 'The paper I mentioned had another word written on it.'

'What?'

'Rustler. Just his name and that word. That was all,' he said stoically. Then he answered the question. 'Me and the three vagrants took the body to the sheriff.'

'Wade? Sheriff Wade?'

'Yes. Why?'

'We've spoken to Sheriff Wade. He denies any knowledge of Joey.'

'Well that's just an out-and-out lie. I was there when he took a look at the body.'

'What happened after that?'

'We took your nephew's body over to Doc Thomas for him to take a look at it.' He shot a sideways glance at Matt. 'Did the doc deny he'd seen him?'

'We haven't been able to speak to the doc as yet.'

'Oh.'

'Tell us about these three . . . *vagrants* I think you called them.'

'I'd never clapped eyes on them before that night. Nor have I since. There's talk that they squat out east of here, near a small ranch. Zeb Grant's place. Not far from the old mine diggings. Dirty bunch. Smell 'em a mile off.'

'They have a name?'

'Ekstold. Or something like that. Old man and two sons. Both a bit simple-minded if you ask me,' he added. 'Scavengers.'

Matt shot out a hand. 'We're much obliged for the information, Mr Stoltz. I guess we'll pay these Ekstolds a visit.'

Harve gave directions, and they set off at a canter. After a couple of miles Matt reined in and stepped down. Bob followed suit.

'So now we know,' he said wryly.

'And,' added Bob, 'we know we've been getting the run-around.'

'Yes. After we've seen Ekstold, I reckon we should have words with the sheriff and then pay the doctor a visit.'

'Yep.'

At the edge of a stream they came across a youth fast asleep under a cottonwood. Matt dismounted and gave his booted foot a kick. The youth woke up fast. Startled, he eyed Matt cautiously.

'What ya wanna go and do that fer?'

Matt ignored his protest. 'I need directions to the Ekstold place.'

'What?'

Although seething inside, Matt repeated his words patiently.

'Oh!' the youth exclaimed. 'My name's Ekstold. Gabriel. Like the angel. Is it me you want?'

'No. Your pa.'

'Oh. Well I'll be headin' thataway soon. You kin foller me.'

Matt kicked his boot again. 'Get on your feet. We're going now.'

'But I ain't finished. . . .'

That was as far as he got with his protest. He gulped at the sight of the Colt in Matt's hand. And when the hammer clicked back, he almost shit his pants.

'Get up, *now*,' Matt commanded.

Gabriel Ekstold got swiftly to his feet. 'You ain't got no call to be nasty,' he said. Then he pointed. 'That's my mule, over there.' The scrawny-looking animal was tethered to a tree; a cow was tied to the mule.

Matt pointed. 'That your cow?'

'Yep.'

'It's got a Triple-Bar 8 brand on it.'

Gabriel knew he'd been caught red-handed. 'I found it, mister. Honest. Found it near Zeb Grant's land. Just takin' it back to 'im.'

'Where is this Zeb Grant's ranch?'

'See that post, mister?' He pointed. 'That's Zeb's boundary.' From not far away came the sound of a decent-sized herd of cattle. Gabriel saw the two men look that way. 'Jez Moxley keeps some of his cows there.'

'On Zeb Grant's land?'

'Yeah. An' Zeb don't mind if we take one every now and again.'

'See that Triple-Bar 8 brand?' Bob whispered.

'What about it?

'It's good work. Professional. But the original brand has been altered. No doubt about it.'

Matt took a closer look. 'You sure?'

'Yep. I'd say the original was Bar C.'

105

'So that's Moxley's game.' Matt turned to Gabriel. 'Take us to your pa.'

They mounted up. 'We'll take a look at a few more of those cows on the way.'

Most of the cattle carried the Bar C, but a good few were branded Triple-Bar 8.

Bob looked at Matt. 'Guess this answers a lot more questions, huh?' he said. Matt nodded.

It wasn't far to Ekstold's camp. The place was well hidden amongst a number of large boulders. A half-built cabin could be seen at the far end of a tiny canyon. Near the entrance two tattered tents were pitched. A small corral was home to a couple of mules and a horse. Chickens squawked loudly, dashing hither and thither, pecking at the dirt. Matt could see a small flock of geese, a few ducks, a lone sheep, and a lot of shit. The old man came up sharp when he saw that two men followed his son into camp. He made a grab for an ancient-looking carbine.

'Let it lie,' Bob called out, his Winchester pointed at the old man's chest. 'Show me your hands.'

Josiah Ekstold raised his empty hands above his head.

Matt stepped down from his horse, trying hard to avoid stepping in the mess that seemed to almost cover the ground. Bob handed the reins of his horse to Gabriel and followed Matt, both picking a none-too-easy path to where the old man waited. Ekstold looked as if he was about to shit his pants when Matt kicked away the carbine, which lay on the ground where the old man had dropped it.

'You won't be needing that,' Matt said. 'Put your hands down. This isn't a robbery.' He looked around the camp, not seeing anything worth stealing.

Josiah relaxed a little. 'What kin ah do fer you fellers?'

'Information,' said Matt.

'Information costs.' The old man had obviously recovered some of his bravado.

Matt raised one foot, resting it on a sawn log, and pushed his hat to the back of his head.

'In this case, it'll be free.'

The old man took Matt's threat without challenge.

'Some weeks ago you and your boys found a body on Copeland's land. A young man. He'd been hanged.'

The old man's face was impassive.

Matt continued: 'You took the body to Prospect Falls.'

'Who says?' Josiah challenged.

'The night guard at the livery stable.' Ekstold stayed silent. 'He says he went with you when you took the body to the sheriff, then to Doctor Thomas's house. You remember?'

Josiah pulled a face and shrugged. 'I'm havin' a lot of trouble rememberin'. You wouldn't have a drink of whiskey on you, would ya? Wet a man's whistle.' He grinned a toothless grin. 'Might help me remember.' ˎ

Gabriel had wandered over and suddenly spoke. 'You remember, Pa. He was just a kid, not much older than me, you said.'

Josiah aimed a swipe at his son's head, but missed. 'You shut your mouth,' he yelled. 'Keep out of this.'

Matt tugged his Bowie knife out of its scabbard, running the edge of the blade menacingly across the palm of his gloved hand.

'Memory can sure play tricks,' he said. 'Hope this knife don't slip out of my hand.'

The old man watched the long broad blade for a split second and decided that cooperation was the best course of action, especially now his stupid son had let the cat out of the bag.

'Mister, you're in luck. My son's words have brought the incident back to me. Yes.' He pondered. 'I recall what happened now. You must excuse my previous behaviour. I'm gettin' old. Things don't come so readily to mind these days.'

Matt put away the knife. 'I want you to tell me and my partner everything you can remember.'

Ekstold told the story exactly as it had happened.

'Any idea who might have done it?'

Ekstold sniffed and rubbed a grubby hand through his coarse beard.

'Ah'd rather not point a finger at anybody, mister, because I didn't see anything of what might've happened before we got there.'

Matt's temper had been increasing steadily with each second since his first hearing that Joey had been lynched. In one fluid movement he leaned forward, pulled the knife from its scabbard again, and grabbed the old man by the frayed lapel of his coat. He slid the knife forward through the beard until its owner jolted upright, feeling the prick of the razor-sharp tip against his scrawny neck.

'Answer my question!' Matt shouted.

Josiah gulped. 'Copeland,' he called out. 'Copeland. Or Moxley. Maybe both of 'em.'

'That's better. Why hesitate?'

'Rumours, mister, rumours. Lots of talk. That kid weren't the first and he won't be the last.'

*

In all his thirty-five years of life Matt Walker had never killed unless out of necessity, not even when he had shot the bandits holding up the stagecoach had he ever taken any joy from killing a man. But now all that had changed. Now all he wanted to do was find the man, or men, responsible for Joey's death, and to kill them in cold blood. An act of ice-cold vengeance. He wasn't proud that he felt this way, but knew he had to face facts. The callous and cold-hearted act of lynching an innocent nineteen-year-old boy was a crime that only a sadistic man with no feelings could commit. Joey Crane was no rustler. Any fool could surely see that plainly. To brand him as such was in itself a horrendous crime.

Yes, thought Matt, I will have revenge, but the lawman within him demanded that he must first find unequivocal proof.

14

Back in Prospect Falls Matt left Bob at the livery stable and went off to seek out the doctor. The doctor's wife told him that her husband had just stepped out.

'You should find him in the Golden Nugget saloon. He plays dominoes once a week,' she said. 'It's just down the street a ways.'

Matt thanked her and made his way to the saloon.

The bar room was bright with the light of lanterns and candelabra. Matt felt many eyes on him as he marched up to the bar.

'What'll it be, stranger?' asked the bartender.

'Beer. I'm looking for Doctor Thomas. Is he here?'

Before the barkeep had chance to answer Matt felt a tap on his shoulder.

'Hey, mister.'

Matt turned. The smiling cowboy facing him was holding a six-gun. It was levelled at Matt's midriff. Matt started to speak, then felt a sudden presence behind him. He instinctively took a half-step forward, his right hand moving down towards the Colt on his hip, but that was as far as he got. He was grabbed in a bear hug, his arms pinned against his sides. He tried to turn his head but was unable to move. He kicked back with his right boot but his foot found nothing but air.

The smiling cowboy smashed the pistol into the side of Matt's head. Someone else pulled his hat down over his eyes. The huge fist came up from below, slamming into Matt's solar plexus, knocking the wind out of him. That pile-driver was followed by a second one. Another punch smashed into his cheek with tremendous force – it was like being hit by a locomotive. As he staggered back against the man holding him tight Matt's knees began to buckle; he tasted blood, felt like bile rising. His tongue ran across his teeth, one felt loose. Another punch landed on his face and he felt himself spiralling downwards into a black pit.

The man holding him let go and Matt's limp body slumped to the sawdust-covered bar-room floor. The two big cowboys responsible for the beating gave Matt a couple of kicks for good measure.

'That's enough,' said Jez Moxley. 'Throw him into the alley.'

Cool night air fanned his face. Matt wanted to wipe away the dirt from his mouth, but found he couldn't move. Strong hands grabbed him under the arms, lifting him to his feet; he feared another beating. Instead he heard Bob's voice.

'That's it, Matt. One step at a time. Come on. You can do it.'

None of the words seemed to be linked together. Matt was half-dragged, half-carried on to the stoop, and eased into a chair. Nothing seemed real. Everything was a haze except the pain – that was real. Every inch of his body burned with pain. Bob knelt in front of him, a blur of a shape.

'What happened?'

Matt heard the words, but had no understanding of what was being said. He just wanted to close his eyes and go to sleep.

'Matt! Who did this to you?'

Matt tried to clear his head, suddenly realizing that Bob was giving him a drink of water, dabbing his swollen face with something wet.

'What happened?'

There were those words again. Matt tried, but could not answer, his addled brain would not allow any words to be formed; in any case his lips were too swollen to open. Then the blackness returned.

'Jez. Come in.' H.J. Copeland stepped to one side to allow his foreman to squeeze past him as he held the door open. 'Please take a seat.' He gestured to a high-backed chair in front of the desk.

Moxley took off his hat and sat down heavily, sensing something bad was in the air. His boss was being too nice and polite.

Copeland closed the door gently and walked round the desk. He sat down, his face filled with apprehension. He looked down at his hands as though not wanting to make eye contact, nervously twisting the large gold signet ring on the third finger of his left hand.

'Jez,' he said in a faltering voice. 'Jez,' he repeated.

'Thanks for coming. I . . . er, wanted you to be the first to know. . . .' He paused, searching for the right words. Jez Moxley had no such difficulty.

'What's up, boss?' His voice sharp.

Copeland tried again. 'I . . . er, have decided to get out of the cattle business.'

Moxley maintained an impassive expression.

Copeland continued: 'I have accepted an offer for the business from an Eastern consortium. It's a good price, but they have indicated that they will be bringing in their own team. A ranch manager and a foreman. They did promise to find a job for you.'

He looked up as Moxley slammed a big fist down hard on the desk.

'So that's it?' he shouted. 'After all I've done for you.' He knew now that the game was up. Time to cash in the chips. Moxley's chair clattered backwards as he leaped to his feet. He aimed another kick at the fallen piece of furniture. His ramrod's violent reaction to the news made Copeland jump.

'Calm down, Jez,' he soothed. 'Don't take it so hard. I'll see you all right.'

Moxley stormed to the door. He turned. 'You know what, H.J.? You're an ungrateful son of a bitch. And one day soon you *will* be very sorry.' His shouted words echoed loudly around the office walls.

The door slammed back on its hinges, causing the walls to shake. Copeland was left to ponder what had happened. He hadn't expected his foreman to be exactly pleased at the news, but neither had he anticipated such hatred.

*

Two hours later, under the canopy of a cobalt-blue sky, a relaxed Jez Moxley sat his horse on a ridge, watching his crew of rustlers get the herd ready for the trail. He smiled confidently to himself at the cleverness of his plan. The steers, once bearing the Bar C brand, were now the Triple-Bar 8 herd.

A couple of his men had voiced the opinion that they thought it foolhardy to undertake this operation so openly. Moxley had quietened them with threats of violence.

'You let me do the worrying,' he had told them. A lot of people had been bribed, their cooperation or silence purchased. All the same, Moxley had taken the precaution of positioning outriders at strategic points where they could warn of any potential trouble. *Expect the best. Plan for the worst,* had always been Moxley's watchword. Today was just the start of another trail drive like the many he had organized before. He had no fears that this one would be any less successful than the previous drives. He fully expected to get over ninety per cent of the herd to its destination. So confident was he that he had decided not to lead this drive. There were other, far richer pickings to be had closer to home.

This was to be the last drive; he was cashing out before the going got too hot. This herd was headed for the railhead at Wichita, not over the Mexican border to Chihuahua as in the past. No. Down south he would only get half of what he could in the USA. He had already sold the herd subject to arrival. A sizeable deposit was now

114

sitting in a Kansas bank, waiting for him to collect.

As things stood, the herd numbered over 700 head of prime beef. He planned to grab a further couple of hundred in the next couple of days, hopefully more, and to change the brand of any Bar C critters en route. He could almost taste the champagne he would soon be drinking.

Once his business with H.J. Copeland was finished, Moxley planned to fake his own death, then ride south, where he would take a riverboat to the coast. From there he would travel to New Orleans before heading north by train to meet the herd at its destination in a couple of months' time. He totted up the figures and worked out that 1,000 steers or so at twenty-five dollars per head would net him well over 25,000 big ones. He sat his horse as relaxed and content as any man had a right to be, watching the riders far away to his left swing towards the low rise where he sat.

'Howdy, boys,' he greeted when the cowboys reached him. 'How many today?'

A tall thin rider wearing a black wide-brimmed hat, crown pointed with a dent on either side, reined in alongside Moxley.

'Howdy, Jez,' he said, tipping his hat back off his face. 'Got forty, maybe fifty head. Jace and Clint are movin' 'em down to the canyon.'

'See anybody?'

'No. Nary a soul. Steers'll be rebranded by the time we get there.' He laughed loudly. 'Ain't this crazy? Copeland's payin' us to steal his own cows.'

'When the boys have finished there, get 'em over to

Zeb's place and make sure all the brands have been changed to Triple-Bar 8 on them cows we got last week.' said Moxley. 'Then move 'em over to the canyon ready for the drive.'

15

'Excuse me, but is your name Matt Walker?'

Matt paused, a spoonful of stew halfway to his mouth, and looked at the gawky young man who had asked the almost whispered question. Matt's lips and the inside of his mouth were still a little swollen after the beating, but he knew he'd been lucky, instinctively curling into a ball to protect his face as much as possible. No one he or Bob had spoken to would admit to knowing who it was that had given Matt the beating. Matt had only seen the man facing him: a stranger he hadn't seen before or since. He had his suspicions, but Sheriff Wade had vouched for Moxley and the rest of the Bar C riders, saying that none of them were in town that night.

The man who had interrupted Matt's meal was extremely tall, stick thin, and dressed in a once smart suit at least one size too large for his slender frame. He fidgeted constantly with the pair of round glasses perched on the end of his long aquiline nose, pushing the frame up towards his large, round, questioning green eyes. When he wasn't touching his glasses, he kept flicking a thick strand of red hair away from his forehead. He was bareheaded, his hair was thinning a little at the temples, his complexion was pale, almost white. In one hand he held an open notebook, in the other a thick pencil; a second pencil was tucked behind one of his large ears.

'Who wants to know?' Matt demanded in a voice designed to give the clear impression that he did not take kindly to being disturbed.

'Mr Walker, my name is Richard C. Nicholls. I am the editor – *proprietor*,' he corrected in a light apologetic tone, 'of the *Prospect Falls Globe.*'

Matt turned back to his food with a perfunctory, 'So?'

The newsman ignored Matt's rudeness. 'May I ask if you would allow me to speak to you?'

'Isn't that what you are doing?' Gingerly, Matt pushed the spoonful of stew into his mouth and tried to chew, wincing as pains he didn't know he had lanced through his mouth.

Nicholls looked more than a little furtive, even nervous. 'The matter on which I wish to speak to you is, shall we say, most delicate.'

Matt pushed the dish aside, realizing he would have to eat soup for a while yet. 'What's it about?' he enquired.

'I would rather not say,' said Nicholls in a hushed tone. 'Perhaps you would be kind enough to come to my office.' He paused briefly. 'When you have finished your meal, of course. It's one block down from your hotel.'

A chair at his elbow scraped noisily on the wooden floorboards, causing the newspaperman to jump.

'Who's this?' asked Bob Crane, sitting down.

Nicholls introduced himself politely. 'For some time I

118

have been gathering information about several criminal acts that have occurred here in Prospect Falls and the surrounding area,' he said eagerly, his previously gentle voice now taking on more spirit, 'concerning the unlawful activities of a number of prominent people.' His eyes were wide, his expression made it clear that he was looking for a response to what he had said.

Matt and Bob stared at him, waiting for more.

Nicholls had originally planned to hold back the names until he felt safe with these two men, whom he knew little about. Now he saw that he needed to go further if he was to seek their help.

'H.J. Copeland,' he said bluntly, 'and his foreman, Jez Moxley.'

Matt's expression asked for more.

'The mayor, the citizen's committee, and Sheriff Wade are also involved,' Nicholls whispered.

'Involved in what, exactly?'

'Murder,' Nicholls whispered the word, 'theft, rustling, perversion of justice. I know of certain people, one in particular, who will testify if they felt it was safe to do so.' Matt and Bob eyed him warily. 'A public spirited person,' he added.

'So?'

'All that is needed is a strong lawman to enforce the subpoenas that could be issued.'

'Sheriff Wade?'

'No! As I said, he is involved. It has to be someone independent.'

Matt suspected what was coming.

'I have done some digging, and have discovered that

you hold the office of marshal.'

So the cat was out of the bag. Matt eyed the young man.

'Town marshal,' he said. 'I have no jurisdiction in New Mexico, or anywhere outside the town where I work.'

As he watched Matt and Bob walk away, the newspaperman's face was filled with disappointment.

Later that afternoon Matt decided to take one last go at Sheriff Wade. He left the hotel, and headed towards Wade's office.

'Mr Walker.'

Matt turned to see Richard Nicholls walking fast after him.

Matt halted and waited for the newsman to catch up.

'Hello again. You are nothing if not persistent,' he greeted. 'You gonna tell me more about your mystery cowboy?'

The newsman looked hurt. 'There is no mystery about him. His name is Jud Heap.'

'Jud Heap?'

'Yes, Mr Walker. May I call you Matt?'

'If you prefer.'

Nicholls looked around furtively. 'Could we speak privately?' he asked, taking hold of Matt's sleeve. 'My office is just down the street. Please?' he added.

Matt decided to listen, and allowed the newspaperman to guide him to his office. Nicholls took out a bunch of keys, selected one and unlocked the door. He stepped to one side, ushering Matt inside.

Once Matt was inside, the newsman locked the door behind him.

'Please take a seat.' He gestured towards an upholstered chair in front of a huge oak desk. Matt watched as Nicholls lit a lantern and pulled down the shades. He was extremely light in his movement, prancing on the balls of his feet like a ballet dancer. The room became dark. The single shaded lantern cast a dim light in one direction, giving the room an eerie glow. Nicholls was obviously extremely nervous. He sat down behind the desk, his eyes flitting about the room nervously.

'Well?' said Matt patiently.

Nicholls hesitated. 'What I am about to tell you is in the strictest confidence.'

'OK.'

'Some weeks ago – it was late one night, I was just finishing up before going home for the evening when there was a knock on the back door. It was one of the Bar C riders. I recognized him but didn't know his name. I'd seen him in the town a number of times. He asked if he could come in, saying that he had a story to tell me that would blow my mind. Before he would enter he asked if I would pull down the window blinds. Only when I had done this did he consent to step across the threshold.'

Matt realized this was going to be a long story. He leaned back into the seat padding and listened patiently.

'You haven't said anything,' Nicholls challenged.

Matt looked him in the eye. 'I'll just listen, if you don't mind. Please continue.'

After a few seconds of silence Nicholls continued with his story, slapping the table with the flat of his hand for emphasis when he finished.

'Did this Jud Heap give you a reason for his betrayal?'

Matt asked.

'Yes. He told me he was seething inside. He'd had a run-in with Copeland's foreman. A roughneck named Jez Moxley.'

'What caused the run-in?'

'Apparently he protested too strongly when Moxley shot his best friend.'

'His best friend?'

'Yes. He also worked for Copeland.' Nicholls paused. 'He was also upset that he hadn't been paid for over three weeks. He said that he and a couple of other Bar C riders suspected that Moxley was holding back their wages. Moxley beat him up in front of the other ranch hands. Then he singled him out again later and beat him again, this time with a shaved-down spoke of a wagon wheel. There have been many instances where things – that was the word he used: *things* – things had been done. Bad things. Things that go against everything a God-fearing person believes in. Things that he and his friend didn't want any part of.'

'What kind of things?'

'He claims to know of three or four lynchings.'

'Lynchings?'

'Drifters. Trespassers on Bar C land who Moxley swore were rustlers.'

'That's quite an allegation.'

'He said he had witnessed one of the lynchings. An innocent young man who was passing through.'

'A young man?'

Nicholls nodded.

'Did the cowboy know his name?' Matt asked.

'He said not. But I think he does.'

'Why?'

'I think he's holding it back. I can't say why. He also told me that Moxley had murdered a Mexican sheepherder and his young son. Some of his sheep had strayed on to Copeland's land. He alleged that Moxley tortured them before he killed them. Moxley hates greasers, he said. Moxley and some other range riders burnt the sheep and the bodies of the two Mexicans. He said that the cowboy who told him this said he couldn't get the stench out of his nostrils.'

'Why single you out to confide in?' Matt challenged.

'He said he figured I was the only man he would trust to do the right thing. He claims that Sheriff Wade is on Copeland's payroll, as is Judge Leach, and that Copeland has the entire town council eating out of the palm of his hand. They are all on the take, according to the cowboy.' He slid open a drawer and took out a piece of paper. 'This is his sworn affidavit. Signed and witnessed by myself and J.J. Sweeney, my typesetter.'

'Where's this cowboy now?'

'He's lying low, but I know where I can reach him when the time is right. He drew me a map with directions to the cabin he's living in.'

'He willing to testify in a court of law?'

'Said so. Also said he could rely on at least one more of Copeland's men to back up his claims. But not if the court is here in Prospect Falls. He doesn't trust anybody in authority in this town.'

'What are you planning to do with this information?'

'I was planning to take Jud to talk to the federal authorities in Santa Fe.'

'Does anyone else know, or suspect you have this information?'

'Not as far as I know.'

'OK. I have one more question.'

'Ask away.'

'Why are you telling *me* this?' asked Matt. Nicholls's face screwed into an expression of puzzlement. 'Aren't you worried that I'll tell Copeland about it?' Matt added. 'I'll bet he'd pay plenty to hear the story.'

Nicholls leaned forward in his chair and stroked his chin. 'I'm sure he would,' he agreed, 'but look. I know you are a lawman. I know where you come from, and I know why you are here. Matt, we have the same goals, you and I. I am certain that Copeland and Moxley are behind the death of your nephew.'

Matt bit his bottom lip. 'We already know about Joey.'

'Yes. But can you prove it?

'No. Not as yet.'

'Don't you see? With Jud Heap's testimony we can prove it. I need you and your brother-in-law to travel with me and the witness to Santa Fe . . .' he saw Matt raised eyebrows, 'in case of trouble,' he finished quickly.

'As protection?'

'You could put it that way. Yes.'

Matt leaned back in his chair. 'I'll need to discuss this with my partner,' he said thoughtfully. What the newsman had said about his nephew was only just beginning to register. 'You say that this Jud Heap will testify that Copeland and Moxley are behind the death of my nephew?'

'Yes, he will,' answered Nicholls, 'I am certain of it.'

Matt's mind went into a sudden turmoil at the revelation.

Until now he had wanted to push every negative thought about Joey to the back of his mind, yet knowing he had finally to accept that his nephew was dead. Matt's throat choked as he told the newsman what Harve Stoltz had said.

'So now we have other corroborating testimony to back up Judd's.'

'How solid is the word of this cowhand?'

'I trust him, if that's what you are asking.' Nicholls nodded, then bucked up when Matt added,

'It'll do for a start.'

The lantern flickered briefly, as though somewhere a door or window had been opened. Matt heard a noise. The faintest of sounds, like wood creaking. His hand dropped to his six-gun. 'Anybody else in this building?'

'Not as far as I know,' Nicholls replied, looking around the room.

'Douse that light,' Matt ordered, sliding back his chair as noiselessly as he could. He eased his pistol out of its holster. 'Stay there,' he said.

Nicholls killed the light, plunging the room into darkness. Matt paused a moment for his eyes to become accustomed to the dark, head tilted to one side, listening for any sound that might explain what had happened. Several rays of moonlight found their way around the edges of the window shades. Not much, but sufficient to enable Matt to see. He pointed a finger at a door.

'What's back there?' he whispered.

'Just a storeroom. I keep it locked,' Nicholls whispered back. He held out a key.

Matt took it and pushed the gun out in front of him. He crossed the room to the storeroom door, holding back a yelp when his knee accidentally collided with some solid object. A thin shaft of light illuminated the door. Matt located the lock and inserted the key. In the silence, the metallic click of the lock sounded like the crack of a bull-whip. Another faint sound came to his ears. A scraping, followed by a dull thud. Matt stood to one side of the door as a precaution against someone firing a shot through the door, grabbed the doorhandle and turned it. More scuffling. Six-gun extended, Matt pushed the door fully open. For a second he stood motionless, bright moonlight streamed through a tiny window, bathing the storeroom in light. His keen eyes searched every corner; boxes and packing-cases were stacked neatly – no one was there. A light breeze fanned his cheek making him turn round to face the window. He saw it was open.

Nicholls appeared at Matt's shoulder. 'What was it?' he asked. 'A rat?'

Matt holstered his gun. 'Window's open.' He pointed. 'I think we have to assume that our conversation was over-heard,' he said ruefully.

'Then there's no time to lose. We need to act.'

'OK,' said Matt, closing the window. 'I'll go track down Bob, and tell him what we are going to do. Pack what you need for a couple of days, and meet me at the livery stable in twenty minutes.'

'OK.'

'Oh. And Nicholls. Bring a gun. Rifle if you've got one.'

'I have.'

Matt found Bob Crane in his room at the Carlton Hotel and in less than ten minutes the two men were in the street, heading for the livery stable. Horses saddled, they waited in the dusty stable for the newspaperman to appear.

Impatiently Bob looked at his pocket watch. 'Think he's had second thoughts?'

'Hope not,' Matt replied, a trace of impatience in his voice. 'But I wouldn't blame him if he had.'

Hands swept down to six-guns as a side-door opened.

'It's me,' a voice whispered. A slender shaft of moon-light illuminated Nicholls's excited face. 'Sorry to have taken so long. I couldn't find my pistol.' He held out the gun for his fellow conspirators to see. It was a huge ancient single-shot cap and ball Dragoon pistol. 'It was my father's,' he told them proudly.

'No time for that,' said Matt. 'Where's your horse?'

'Outside the side door,' Nicholls replied.

'OK, let's get going.'

Bob reached out and grabbed the handle on the main door. The wood creaked loudly, then the door banged shut with a sound like an explosion when a sharp gust of wind snatched the handle from Bob's grasp. He grabbed it again, this time managing to hold the door open wide enough for Matt to lead the horses through.

'Sorry,' he apologized. They led the horses round the side of the building, and mounted.

'Which way,' Matt asked the newspaperman.

'North.'

'OK. Down the alley,' said Matt. 'We'll circle around back of the buildings, walk the horses. Don't want to create any interest in our leaving.'

In less than five minutes the three riders broke into a gallop.

16

In the back room of his office Sheriff Wade tossed back a second large glass of red-eye. The alcohol didn't take away the pain of surrendering his self-respect, but at least it helped. Hearing a tapping on the window pane, he turned. The top of a kid's head bobbed up and down, in and out of sight. Wade blinked a couple of times before his brain registered what he was seeing. He got up from his chair and unlocked the back door.

Facing him was a twelve-year-old boy, lanky, tall for his age, with an unruly mop of straggly straw-coloured hair. The boy held out one hand, palm upward.

'I got valuable information for you, Sheriff.'

Wade tilted his head to regard the boy. 'How much?'

'A dollar,' replied the grim-faced urchin. 'It's worth more,' the boy added quickly.

Sheriff Wade eyed the child for a moment. The kid was well known around town for getting into a multitude of scrapes.

'OK,' he said, fishing out two fifty-cent coins. One he pressed into the boy's hand. 'You'll get the other after you tell me this *valuable* information,' he emphasized the word.

For a moment, the boy looked disappointed, then shrugged. 'OK,' he agreed.

Sheriff Wade listened patiently while the boy told him what he had heard, punctuating the story with sounds of exclamation and the occasional 'what?'

The boy deliberately left out how he came to have been in the storeroom of the newspaper office, and why.

'You done good, lad,' said the sheriff, handing over the second coin. He patted the boy on the shoulder. 'Now get out of here. And make sure you don't tell anybody else about this.'

The boy grinned and turned to leave. Wade aimed a playful cuff at the back of the kid's head as he opened the door. The kid ran out into the street, happily jingling the coins in his pocket.

Sheriff Wade returned to his desk and drained the tumbler. He picked up the bottle of whiskey and poured another stiff one, sipping it while he pondered long and hard about what to do with his newly purchased knowledge. Normally he wouldn't have hesitated for a second before riding out to the Bar C to tell Copeland. But after the way the rancher had treated him earlier, why should he bother to make the long ride? He decided to tell Jez Moxley. *He* could tell Copeland. Wade had seen the big Bar C ramrod earlier in the evening in the Golden Nugget saloon, drinking with four or five of his gang. Wade grabbed his hat and headed across the street.

'What?' shouted Jez Moxley when the sheriff told him what had happened. 'Jud Heap! That no-good yeller-bellied skunk. I knew it. He always was a double-crossin' snake.'

'What you gonna do?' Wade asked.

'Kill him,' Moxley snarled. 'Rode north, you say?' Wade nodded. 'Then I know exactly where he'll be. We gotta stop him from gettin' to Santa Fe.' He turned to his men. 'Get the horses. We got some killin' to do.'

The tiny shack, its walls of rough sawn logs, its roof a patchwork of wooden tiles, moss and grass, sat in a small steep-sided bowl shaped valley against a sheer fifty-foot high rocky cliff. The area in front of the cabin was flat and well grassed, having been cleared of trees and brush many years earlier. In places there was evidence that Mother Nature was striving hard to reclaim the land ravaged by mankind. To the left of the cabin a small corral held one horse. To the right a pond shimmered, its surface rippled by dripping water from a cleft high up on the cliff face. The valley slopes were covered with dense forest, interspersed with rocky outcrops.

Matt Walker reined in his horse on the steep trail high above the floor of the clearing, Bob Crane and Richard Nicholls alongside him. No smoke came from the rock-built chimney. If it wasn't for the horse Matt would have sworn it had been a long time since the place had been inhabited. The three man team moved cautiously down a severely overgrown shale-covered trail that zigzagged around boulders and trees to the bottom of the valley.

The procession halted at the foot of the slope; the outline of the cabin was clearly visible through the trees. What looked like the barrel of a rifle poked through a window. Nicholls held up a hand to call a halt to their progress. Bob held back behind a rocky outcrop until they were sure of the welcome waiting for them.

The newspaperman cupped his hands and called out.

'Jud! Jud Heap! It's me, Richard Nicholls. I have friends with me.' When no answer came, the newspaperman repeated his call.

A metallic click behind him brought Nicholls's head round fast. He found himself staring down the barrel of a six-gun.

'Jud!' he exclaimed, seeing who was holding the gun.

The cowboy spoke. 'Who's this?' Without waiting for an answer he turned to Matt. 'Stay right still, mister. And keep your hands where I can see 'em.'

Matt smiled inwardly. It was as though he and Bob had read the script in the cowboy's mind. Any trace of satisfaction on the part of Jud Heap disappeared when he felt the prod of a pistol in the small of his back.

'Drop it,' ordered Bob Crane.

Jud had heard no sound behind him before feeling the pressure of the gun. He allowed the Colt to slip from his grasp and raised his hands.

Bob holstered his pistol. 'OK, young feller. You can put your hands down.

Puzzled by the words, Jud Heap turned round. 'Who are you, mister?'

Bob tipped his hat back to the back of his head. 'A friend,' he said.

The newspaperman interrupted. 'Jud. It's me, Richard Nicholls. Didn't you hear me call out to you?'

'No. I heard horses and figured it might be Moxley.'

Nicholls made a sound designed to indicate that he

131

understood the wisdom of always checking who it was that came calling, when Matt interrupted.

'Does Copeland know about this place?' he asked.

'No, but I think Moxley might.'

'How come?'

'It was one of the longer-serving Bar C riders who told me about this place. Moxley's gang used it years ago before he moved his operation nearer the border.'

Bob couldn't believe anybody could be so naïve. 'Doesn't strike me as the safest place to hide out if the man you're hiding from knows the place.'

From the surprised look on Jud Heap's face Bob doubted that the cowboy had ever thought about that.

The newspaperman explained his plan.

'Better get mounted and get out of here,' said Matt.

Jud retrieved his pistol from where it had fallen, giving the gun a wipe on his sleeve before sliding it into its holster.

'I'll get my stuff,' he announced.

'I'll saddle your horse,' offered Matt as they made their way to the cabin. 'We better take another trail out of here.'

'There ain't one,' Jud piped up. 'The way you came in is the only way out.'

'Then we better be extra vigilant. Could be Moxley's not far behind us.'

'Be dark in a coupla hours,' Bob observed. 'I suggest we ride all night. Put as much distance between us and this place as is possible.'

'Wind's getting up. Could be a storm's on the way.'

Heading south, the four riders urged their horses up the steeply sloping trail out of the valley. At the top of the

132

slope Jud Heap turned in the saddle.

'We can turn west in a mile or two. There's an old trail. Then in another few miles we'll hit the road north to Santa Fe.'

'Sooner the better,' Nicholls commented with a shiver; there was a nervous edge to his voice.

The rising wind brought a chill to the air. Dark clouds scuttled across the sky. The rough trail followed the bed of a dried-up stream, and continued through a narrow defile. It wasn't possible to move at a fast pace on this section of their journey, and more than once they were forced to walk their horses.

Jud Heap rode spur to spur with Bob Crane whenever the trail allowed, with Matt and Nicholls bringing up the rear. In a small stand of cottonwoods Bob held up a hand and reined in his mount; his horse snorted in protest as the bit was pulled tight.

'What is it?' Matt whispered.

'Might be something. Might be nothing,' Bob said softly. 'I got one of my uneasy feelings.'

A bullet brought down a scattering of leaves as it passed near by. A split second later the loud report of a rifle rang out.

'Down!' Bob shouted.

The four men flung themselves from their saddles.

'Hold on to your horses,' Matt shouted as two of the mounts reared up.

More shots rang out, bringing down more leaves and foliage.

Bob sidled over to where Matt was levering a round into the chamber of his Winchester. 'They're up there in those rocks.' He pointed. 'I'd say four or five of 'em, using repeaters.'

Matt nodded. 'Think we can flush 'em out?'

'Won't be easy,' Bob answered. 'Think you can draw their fire?'

Matt shot a sideways glance at Bob. 'You gonna try to out flank 'em?'

'Yep.' Bob turned to the cowboy and the newspaper-man. 'I need you two to set up a steady rate of fire into those rocks up there on that ridge. Move position when you can, and try to keep your heads down. Think you can do it?'

The two men said they'd try.

'The good news,' said Bob, 'is that they're at the extreme end of their range.'

'Let's just hope they ain't got a big-bore buffalo gun with them,' said Matt, hunkering down, his back against a broad tree-trunk.

Bob led the other two a little way along the trail. The two men squirmed along behind a large boulder. Bullets whined as they ricocheted off the granite rocks. Matt slid along after Bob and the others.

'You ready?' Matt called across to Bob.

'No!' he answered with a smile.

Matt took off his hat, balanced it on the end of a long stick, then raised it above the level of the boulder. The Stetson flew backwards as a fusillade of bullets struck it. Gun flashes on the ridge were visible in the growing gloom. Bob and Matt fired off a couple of shots.

'They've set up a crossfire. We need to get out of here,' Bobe called out as a stream of bullets crashed around him.

134

Matt turned. 'You two, take the horses back through the trees a coupla hundred yards.' He was on his knees tugging his Sharps out of its holster. 'I'll keep 'em busy with this.' He grabbed a box of shells.

Bob fired round after round until the barrel of his Winchester was too hot to hold. The sound of the four horses being led away diminished. He looked across at Matt, who was fixing the telescoping sight to the Sharps.

'You ready?' Matt slid a shell into the breech.

'Ready as I'll ever be,' he said stoically, pushing the big gun through a small cleft in the rocks. He sighted through the gap, and adjusted the sights. 'OK,' he said.

Bob took that as his signal to fire off a shot, knowing it would be answered. Matt sighted on the muzzle flash, waited for a moment, then squeezed the trigger. He didn't know it but his bullet had hit the shooter clean through one eye. Matt repeated the procedure with one of the bushwhackers on the flank. Then twice more at both locations. For a moment all went silent. Matt guessed that his shooting had given the ambushers something to think about. Two more shots and he and Bob high-tailed it out of there, trying not to trip over a tree root or get their rifles caught between their legs. Fortunately they didn't have to run far: fifty yards down the track the newspaperman was waiting with their horses.

Matt holstered the Winchester and Sharps and swung into the saddle.

'Where's Jud?' he asked.

'He went on ahead to make sure the trail is clear,' replied Nicholls.

At the turn-off to the cabin in the valley the three riders

encountered Jud coming fast from the other direction.

'Riders comin'. Down the slope,' he said. 'Saw 'em from the crest of that ridge.' He pointed into the distance. 'Bar C cowboys. No doubt. I recognized a couple of the horses.'

'How many?'

'Six. Maybe seven.'

'Plus four or five behind us, depending upon how many Matt managed to put down,' Bob said. 'Reckon them bushwhackers will be on our heels pretty soon.' He turned to Jud. 'We've no chance out here in the open. Which is the shortest way out of here?'

'There ain't one,' Jud Heap replied. 'This is the only trail I know of.' He shrugged. 'Our best chance is to get back to the cabin.'

'Better than nothin',' answered Bob. 'It's a good defensive position. Sheer cliff at the back. Good water. How far's that ridge stretch?'

'Miles,' Jud answered. 'Take a fast rider with a good horse half a day to reach the place where it flattens down enough to get up it. The cabin's got plenty of supplies. I know, 'cos I ferried 'em there.'

'Let's go,' shouted Matt.

17

'Horses in the corral,' Matt shouted the order. 'Leave 'em saddled. Bring all the guns and ammunition. Let's get inside.'

Bob stopped abruptly.

'I got an idea.' To Matt he said, 'Bring the Sharps and your Winchester, plus plenty of ammunition. I got a hankerin' to ambush, them bushwhackers.' To Nicholls and Jud Heap he said, 'You two get inside the cabin and get ready. Light the lamps and get a fire going.'

'That's crazy,' Nicholls protested. 'They'll know exactly where we are.'

'Correct,' said Bob. 'I want them to think we're all in there. Keep well away from the windows. Matt and I will set up an ambush at the top of the tree line.' The army scout looked across at Matt. 'Hope to take out a few of 'em on the trail, but when the going gets too hot we'll leg it back to the cabin. That'll be your cue to set up a good rate of fire.'

The newspaperman and the cowhand protested strongly, saying they wanted to be part of the ambush. Matt persuaded them to get inside the cabin. Then he and Bob grabbed their weapons and jogged back up the trail and into the trees.

The darkening sky had cleared, the earlier clouds having been blown away by the wind. Under a starlit canopy the two men selected good positions above the narrow winding trail, where an outcrop of granite would force their foe to slow their horses to a walk, and from where they could fire down on their attackers. Matt lay in a shallow depression. He pulled up the collar of his coat against the cold and thought through the merit of Bob's plan. Once the file of men got into the open, Matt would shoot the riders at the front of the file. Bob would concentrate his fire on the men and horses at the rear, effectively blocking their advance and retreat.

Neither man relished the notion of shooting innocent horses, but knew they had no alternative. There would be no time for second thoughts, and both men would have to shoot fast. With luck they would get four or five of the gang before Moxley realized what was happening. The two men levered rounds into the chambers of their weapons and settled down to wait.

In less than ten minutes the first rider appeared in the gap between the steeply sloping sides of the trail. A big man on a big horse. The second man was even bigger. Matt figured him to be the foreman of the Bar C: Jez Moxley. The two riders halted, obviously cautious. The lead man pointed down towards the depths of the valley. Through the trees a pinprick of light showed clear in the darkness.

Moxley drew back, sending two men on ahead. To

another he said, 'You go round and get up on that ridge. Take Lefty with you.'

'Aw, Jez, it'll take forever to get up there,' the cowboy protested.

'Just do it,' Moxley growled. 'I don't want them gettin' away that way. If any of 'em try climbin' out of there, you and Lefty start shootin'.'

Through a telescope from his elevated position high above the narrow trail, Bob Crane watched Jez Moxley motion two of his riders to move ahead. Bob and Matt had chosen well-hidden positions that gave a commanding view of the trail.

Matt rested the heavy octagonal barrel of the big Sharps .50-90 in a groove in a large rock, lining the sights on a spot on the trail he'd marked in his head.

Completely unaware that they were being watched, the two leading cowboys eased their mounts to the spot. The other riders following at a considerable distance behind in single file. Matt took aim at the leading rider and squeezed the trigger. The shot rang out loudly, and the lead rider was thrown backwards from the saddle. In a split second Matt had reloaded and fired off a second shot. The horse immediately behind the first squealed and reared, pitching its rider to the ground. The third horse screamed and fell heavily, its rider with it. From the man's scream Matt figured the rustler's leg must have been busted by the weight of the horse falling on him.

High above the head of the trail, Winchester levelled, Bob Crane heard Matt's first shot and downed the horse and rider at the rear of the line. Several answering shots zipped past near by, a couple slamming into the trunks of trees; others ricocheted from rocks with a whine. Below him on the narrow valley trail terrified horses whinnied and screamed, rearing, their riders frantically trying to dismount and find cover.

Bob's plan was working perfectly; the tight trail was blocked; there was no way forward or back. In the centre of the mêlée confused men and horses milled around, sending up clouds of dust from the sun-baked earth.

Matt discarded the Sharps in favour of the Winchester and began firing indiscriminately. He knew Bob would be doing the same. Bullets whined over Matt's head, until Moxley's gruff voice was heard.

'Hold your fire,' he screamed at his men. 'Don't waste your ammo.'

The dust cloud began to disperse, and suddenly there was no one to shoot at; Moxley and his gang had found cover. A couple of wounded horses still squealed with pain until one or more of the cowboys put the animals out of their misery. The rustler with the broken leg had disappeared, along with all but one of the dead bodies. Matt figured that between him and Bob they had downed four, maybe five rustlers, any number of whom might still be capable of firing a gun. That meant they were still outnumbered, but at least the odds had moved considerably in their favour. Moxley and the remaining members of his gang were pinned down behind a group of boulders.

Matt moved position again, his third in as many minutes, dropping down nearer the level of the trail. Through the rocks and bushes he caught a fleeting glimpse of Bob, he too was moving to a new position.

Twenty or so feet below, the crown of a battered Stetson rose slowly above a boulder, Matt took quick aim and fired. The bullet tore through the hat, carving a hole through its owner's forehead: another one down.

Jez Moxley watched as the body of the man next to him was flung back by the force of a slug. He realized he was not in a good place.

'Tex? Tex?' he called out in a hushed voice.

Tex's face was set in the grim expression of death, lifeless eyes staring vacantly, his mouth open, but unable to speak.

'We gotta get outa here,' Moxley yelled, seeing another of his men clutch at his bloodstained chest. 'They're pickin' us off one by one.' His brain whirred, trying to come up with a plan. Suddenly he called out again.

'We'll use the horses to shield us. Jake, can you reach 'em if we give you cover?'

'I can try,' Jake answered grimly.

Moxley nodded. 'On the count of three. One . . . two . . . three.'

On three, Moxley and the rest of his gang sprayed the slope with a stream of bullets, levering shell after shell into the chambers of their rifles until the barrels almost glowed. The answering fire kept Matt and Bob's heads down long enough for Jake to gather up the trailing reins of the horses, and calm the skittish animals a little. The remaining rustlers crouched low behind the horses as Jake led the way back up the sloping trail.

A shot rang out and another horse went down. Bob hated shooting horses, but there was no other choice. Seeing what was happening Moxley leaped on to the back of his horse and dug his spurs in deep, bending low, six-guns in each hand barking out an invitation to death. His horse raced away up the slope. Others followed his lead, guns spewing out lead at the unseen shooters, horses having to leap over the fallen animals further up the trail.

Four rustlers made it out of that valley of death. The others who tried to make it out on horseback lay in the dust, left for dead by their fleeing comrades.

Moxley's move had taken Matt and Bob by surprise; they hadn't wanted to let Copeland's big ramrod get away. Still, they were safe now, or should be. But first there was the task of taking care of the wounded rustlers, making certain they were disarmed.

In a loping crouch Matt moved cautiously down the slope to a clump of grey boulders. He had almost made it when a bare-headed man rose up from the rocks away to his right. Matt realized that some of the rustlers, left behind by Moxley, must have tried to get behind him. The man was aiming a rifle at something directly ahead of him.

Suddenly Matt's boot found a dry twig. The snap brought the rustler round to face him, rifle raised ready to fire. Without hesitation Matt fired his Winchester from the hip, then dipped behind a boulder as he heard the man cry out. Matt raised his head sufficiently to see the man fall forward clutching at the crimson stain spreading across his breast. His lifeless body slid puppet-like down the rocks.

Another rustler appeared, coming towards Matt at the run, six-gun in hand, spraying unaimed bullets that whined and ricocheted in all directions. Matt was about to fire, when he heard the report of a rifle shot further to his right. The man fell headlong, blood streaming from a hole in his temple.

Breathing deeply, Matt altered his position, hoping there weren't any others around. He leaned his back against the trunk of a large cedar tree to get his breath back. Hearing a noise he spun around, coming face to face with a young cowpoke not a yard away – couldn't have been much older than twenty. Matt had his empty Winchester out in front of him, the young man too was pointing an unloaded rifle.

Matt reacted first, bringing his rifle up on to that of his opponent, knocking the weapon to the ground. He side-swiped with the Winchester as the kid went for the six-shooter holstered on his hip; the barrel bounced off the kid's arm to catch his wrist. Several shots rang out as the kid drew a long knife, and lunged forward. Matt rammed the Winchester into the kid's midriff, then crashed the butt of the rifle on the youth's head.

A bright moon came out from behind the clouds, bathing the valley in a silvery light as Matt thumbed shells into the Winchester. Suddenly two men rushed Matt's position, zigzagging as much as the terrain would allow; another man limped along behind. Matt took aim at the closer man and fired, his first bullet dropping the man leading the charge.

The second man dropped like a stone as a bullet from an unseen gun took him in the gut. The limping man shot first, but missed. Matt dived sideways, firing as he went. His bullet took the rustler in the chest. All went strangely quiet.

'Reckon he was the last of 'em.'

Matt glanced sideways to see Bob not ten yards away, a still smoking Winchester in his hand.

As the four men mounted up Matt told Nicholls and Jud Heap: 'You shouldn't have any trouble getting to Santa Fe now. Bob and I will go after Moxley.'

At the head of the trail Nicholls held out a hand.

'I want to thank both of you. Without your help this would not have been possible.'

Bob tipped his hat.

'Good luck,' said Matt.

'Good luck to you too,' replied Nicholls.

18

A sweating Jez Moxley removed his spurs before entering the ranch house and trod inside as lightly as he could. It had been a hard ride from the disaster at the cabin, each stride of his horse filled his heart with hatred for those who had so effectively ambushed him and his men. He couldn't be certain, but he figured that the shooters were those two nosy relations of that kid he'd lynched. What had happened had only served to speed up the chain of events he had already planned for.

Moxley moved like a cat as he made his way through the ranch house. He closed the door gently behind him. H.J. Copeland was sitting at his desk, poring over a pile of invoices, unaware of the presence of his ramrod. He didn't hear a thing until the metallic click of the hammer on Moxley's six-gun assailed his ears. H.J. tilted his head slightly to look in the direction of the sharp, unmistakable sound. He saw the Colt in Moxley's big hand. He glanced from the six-gun to his foreman's dark face.

'Jez!' he exclaimed, puzzled to see the gun pointing at his chest. 'You startled me. I didn't hear you come in.'

Moxley said nothing, his face set with grim determination.

Copeland pointed a finger. 'What's that for?'

For a moment Moxley just stared at his boss, as though trying to formulate the words he wanted to say. Then the big man found his voice.

'I need you to open the safe,' he said firmly.

Copeland jolted upright. 'What?'

Moxley pushed the gun forward. 'I said, open the safe.'

Copeland lifted a hand and stroked his chin. 'What if I don't?' he challenged. 'You gonna shoot me?'

'If I have to,' Moxley threatened through gritted teeth.

H.J's face took on a perplexed expression. 'You'd shoot *me* after all I've done for you?'

'I will if I have to. Now quit jawing and open the safe.'

H.J's fist banged on the desk. 'I lifted you out of the gutter, you no good punk. Gave you back your pride. You were just a no-good bum when I found you.'

'You've had more than your pound of flesh out of me, H.J. Now it's over. Open the safe,' Moxley repeated. He took a couple of steps forward and pressed the end of the barrel of the Colt against Copeland's forehead.

'Open it. *Now!*' he yelled.

'If you kill me, Jez, you'll never get the safe open.'

Moxley moved the gun to one side. The flicker of a sneer appeared around H.J's mouth, immediately disappearing when the ramrod whipped the gun barrel across his cheek. Blood spurted from Copeland's nose and lip, the force of the blow propelling him backwards off his chair.

Moxley followed up with a swift kick to Copeland's midriff.

146

'Open it now or I'll give you more pain than you could ever know.' He poked his boss's leg with a booted foot. 'It's your choice, H.J. I can blow it open if I have to. There's dynamite in the shed.'

Copeland spat out a tooth and grabbed the corner of the desk. He hauled his pain-filled body off the floor on to the chair. He was no hero, but he was stubborn. He shook his head, a moment or two before the barrel of the Colt swept down again, this time smashing into his mouth.

Copeland spat out another bloody tooth and held up a hand in surrender. He knew when he was beaten.

'OK. OK,' he cried out, taking a handkerchief from his pocket and dabbing it on his wounds, 'I'll open it. But you better ride far, because I swear I'll get you for this. You know I never make idle threats.'

He struggled to his feet and staggered over to the huge safe standing against the opposite wall. He went down on one knee and operated the combination. He turned his head to face Moxley. 'You absolutely sure you want to go through with this?'

Jez Moxley sneered back. 'Sure. I bin doin' your dirty work for years. You owe me big time.'

'You were paid.'

'Not enough.'

Copeland pulled the safe door open and half turned. He held out a wad of banknotes.

'There's about five thousand dollars there,' he mumbled, his lips beginning to swell up.

Moxley kicked a bag towards his boss. 'I'm taking it all. Put it in that bag.'

Copeland pulled the bag to him and reached into the safe.

'Moxley, you're just a no-good bum,' he said over his shoulder.

'What's that make you?' the ramrod said. 'All the people I killed for you.'

H.J. Copeland swung round suddenly, a pistol in his hand, cocked.

Two shots rang out in the ranch house office. Copeland was flung backwards by Moxley's .45 calibre bullet. The hole dead centre in his forehead oozed blood.

Moxley holstered his Colt and went down on one knee. Henry Copeland's dead eyes stared at him as he cleaned out the contents of the safe, stuffing all the banknotes and papers into the bag. His forearm stung, blood seeped through his shirtsleeve. He rolled back the cuff, relieved to see it was just a flesh wound; Copeland's bullet had only grazed the skin just below his elbow. He retrieved Copeland's handkerchief and wrapped it around the wound. Holding one end in between his teeth he tied a double knot, then picked up the bag and headed for the door.

Outside, Kid Nash held the horses.

'I heard shots. Any trouble?'

Moxley grinned. 'No trouble,' he said mounting his horse. 'Let's go.'

'We headin' for Devil Canyon?'

'Yeah. We'll drive the rest of the cows over the border an' sell 'em. Find somewhere quiet. Lay low for a while with some good tequila and a couple of pretty *señoritas* each. Live the life of rich men.'

148

'Like your thinkin',' said Nash.

Since the thwarted stagecoach robbery, and the botched attempt at killing Jud Heap, Moxley's gang had been severely depleted: he and only three others were left. Moving a few hundred head of beeves across the border would be hard graft for four men, but Moxley knew they would make it. Who was there to stop him? He planned to tell the other three that there had been close to $3,000 in Copeland's safe. He laughed out loud – in reality there had been more than $20,000. After the sale of the rustled cattle he would have more than enough to buy a good-sized spread of his own. Things were definitely looking rosy.

'What's up?' asked Nash.

'Just smiling at our good fortune,' Moxley replied. Deep down, changing his plans galled him. He knew the price of beef in Mexico was well short of what he would have got in Kansas.

The two brothers-in-law rode south from Prospect Falls, Bob taking the lead, Matt leading the pack animals, the hearts of both men filled with thoughts of vengeance. In Mrs Healey's café they had rested only long enough to eat a plate of stew and to drink a couple of cups of hot coffee. Both were tired, near to exhaustion as were their horses, but were driven on by the need to see the men responsible for Joey's death brought to justice. By mid-morning they had reached the banks of the Rio Diablo, a fast flowing tributary of the Rio Grande. The wide river was in flood.

'They turned their horses east,' said Bob, pointing to a

number of tracks, 'headed towards those hills.' They spurred their horses into a gallop.

Nearer the foothills the ground turned rockier, which made finding horse tracks much more difficult. Daylight began to fade as dark clouds crowded the sky.

On a small rise Bob held up a hand and halted. He pointed down the valley to a dried out wash.

'If I was them that's the way I'd go,' he said. 'Follow me.'

To their left, smooth-faced boulders jutted out from gigantic rock formations, interspersed with stands of pine and cedar. It began to rain, lightly at first, then much more heavily. Bob reached back and pulled his slicker from behind his saddle. He shook the garment out and put it on. Matt did the same. The cloudburst didn't last long.

When they were 500 yards into the wash the cutting split into two gullies. One fork had the trickle of a small stream meandering down its centre. On the opposite bank, the tracks of four horses were clear in the mud.

Bob pointed into the distance to where a black mass of trees covered the steep slopes on either side of the valley.

'That way,' he pronounced, spurring his horse into a trot. The wash narrowed considerably the nearer they got to the trees. 'I reckon they'll make camp on the other side of that rocky ridge.'

'What makes you so sure?' Matt challenged, easing his horse alongside Bob's.

'Because that's where I would.'

Matt looked at the scout with a slightly puzzled expression.

'Horses need a rest. So do they,' said Bob.

Matt knew better than to continue questioning Bob's figuring.

'We'll make camp over there. On this side,' Bob said. 'Good water and cover. No fire,' he warned.

After the horses were picketed Matt handed Bob a pack containing bread, meat and cheese.

'Compliments of Mrs Healey,' he said. 'She passed them to me when you were getting set.'

'Much obliged to her and you.'

The two men ate in silence. When the meagre meal was finished Bob rolled a smoke and puffed away. He drained his cup and turned to Matt.

'You a bit sweet on that gal?'

'Who?'

'Mrs Healey?'

Matt shrugged. 'I don't know why you would say that. I hardly know her.'

'Good lookin'. Man could do a lot worse.'

'You trying to get me married off?' Matt chuckled.

'Nope. Just wondered where she fits into your future plans. That's all.'

Matt shook his head. 'I have no plans other than to finish this job and get back to Sweetwater Springs.'

'The hell you say?' Bob stubbed out his cigarette. 'Well, if it ain't Mrs Healey, you got any notions about that Mexican gal?'

The question startled Matt. 'Elena?'

'That's her.' Bob grinned. 'Kinda sweet on you, I'd say. The way that gal looked at you when we left Hector's ranch, all moon eyes. Why, it was pure love.'

'Quit riling me, will you? We got work to do and it

doesn't include any women.'

'OK.' Bob grinned. 'Let's get over that hill before we lose any more of this light.'

They left the horses picketed and made their way to the summit on foot, reaching the crest after a strenuous climb. In the distance small wisps of wood-smoke rose above a dense group of pines.

'That'll be their camp,' said Bob. 'We'll come up on 'em from downwind so they won't hear us till it's too late. Follow me.'

The climb down proved to be harder than the ascent. Knees aching, Bob estimated that they were still over 500 yards from Moxley's camp when somewhere in the distance away to their right a faint whinny sounded clear in the otherwise still evening. The two men went to ground. Bob shrugged, motioning with his head.

'Sound came from over there. Not one of theirs, that's sure.

Matt bit his bottom lip. 'Let's keep going,' he whispered. 'Maybe they won't have heard it.'

They soon reached the edge of the tree line, on the west side of a clearing. Huddled around a blazing campfire in the centre of the clearing two men were drinking coffee, faces bathed in the glow of the flames. Another man was leaning against the trunk of a tree, eating the last mouthfuls of a plate of beans. Standing by the tethered horses was the bulky figure of Jez Moxley. He was examining something in one pocket of a saddle-bag.

Through a break in the trees Matt watched and waited. He shook the tension out of his hands and arms and raised his Winchester to his left shoulder, sighting on the

man standing nearest the horses. Two yards to his right
Bob took aim at one of the two men huddled around the
fire. A cool evening breeze fanned Matt's cheek, the heady
scent of pine was in his nostrils.

'How do you want to play this?' he asked in a low voice.

'I'm thinking on it. Give me a minute,' Bob replied.
'You got any serious ideas?'

Before either of them could say more, from the opposite side of the clearing a clear voice rang out in the
stillness.

'You in the camp. Raise your hands. You are sur-
rounded.'

The words echoed around the clearing. One of the
horses near Moxley reared suddenly, head high in the air,
straining to free itself from its tether. A flock of resting birds
rose as one from the trees into the crimson-streaked sky.

The man eating the beans decided to make a fight of it.
He dropped his plate and went for his gun, Moxley did the
same. A single shot rang out clear in the night air. The
man's Colt didn't clear the holster before he pitched
forward, a bullet in the side of his temple. Moxley fired off
a shot at the unseen assailants as he dived for cover behind
a fallen tree. The two rustlers near the fire also managed
to squeeze off a shot before they too were cut down.
Blindly Moxley fired shot after shot into the trees.

Bob and Matt watched the scene unfold.

Moxley reloaded and yelled out. 'Who's out there?' No
response came, so Moxley repeated his shouted question.
Hidden behind the fallen log Moxley snaked out an arm
to grab a burning log from the fire. He hurled it into the
trees.

By its light Bob saw the shadowy outline of two men. It looked as though someone else was out for revenge.

Moxley reached out again and grabbed another flaming torch from the fire, hurling it after the first. It was almost the last action he would take in his life. A bullet smashed into his shoulder. A second got him in the hand. His Colt tumbled from his grasp across the fallen tree.

One more bullet smacked into the log, sending up a shower of wood chips.

'OK,' Moxley called out. 'OK. I said, I surrender.'

'Stand up. Hands in the air,' the voice from the trees commanded.

Moxley got slowly to his feet as a man stepped out of the trees, the muzzle of a rifle pointing at Moxley's broad chest.

'My shoulder,' Moxley cried out defiantly, taking a step forward. 'I've been hit.'

'Don't move,' the stranger ordered.

Suddenly, in one movement Moxley dived sideways, pulling a six-gun from the back of his belt. He died in mid-air before he could get off a shot, killed by a single bullet from an unseen rifle. This other man now stepped from the trees.

Without showing himself Bob called out at the top of his voice. 'Don't shoot, mister. Me and my partner have got you covered.'

The two men in the clearing froze, their rifles aimed in the general direction of Bob's shout. Bob moved several feet to his right.

'Like I said,' he called out, 'don't shoot. Me and my pard are after Moxley and his gang, but you beat us to it.'

'Who are you, mister?'

'Name's Bob Crane. My pard is Matt Walker. A lawman from Arizona.'

'Step out of the trees where we can see you.'

'After you give me your names.'

'I'm Joe Stanton,' came the reply. He nodded his head to the other man. 'My brother, Mike. You sure you ain't Moxley's men?' he challenged.

'If we were with Moxley we'd have blasted the pair of you as soon as you showed yourselves.'

'Guess you would've at that.' Joe Stanton smiled, lowering his rifle. 'It seems we have a situation here.'

Bob Crane left the trees and walked across the clearing to where Mike Stanton was gathering up the guns and checking that all the rustlers were dead.

Joe squatted near the fire. He reached out a hand to feel the coffee pot.

'Cup of coffee while we talk it over?' he asked. 'Still warm.'

'Sure. Why not?' Bob answered, guardedly. He took the cup Joe Stanton held out.

'You the law?' Stanton asked.

Bob shook his head. 'Uh-uh.' The coffee was bitter. 'You?'

Joe Stanton shook his head.

'So what's your interest in Moxley?'

Stanton tipped back his Stetson. 'We were hired by Copeland to find out who was rustling his cattle, and put a stop to it.'

'So you're working for Copeland?'

'Was, till Moxley shot and killed him dead. Cleared out

155

his safe.' He shrugged. 'Copeland had already paid us, so it was only right we finished the job. Moxley and his crew had been rustling Bar C stock for years.'

'Well, you sure finished it. How did you get ahead of us?'

'Didn't know you were on Moxley's trail. We had found out about this meeting place – trailed another of his boys here a couple of nights ago. There's a few hundred head of cattle in a box canyon a mile or so due south of here. Mostly Bar C, but some are branded with the letter C inside a diamond.'

'Diamond C,' said Bob. 'Belongs to a friend of ours, Hector Cervantes.'

'Mexican?'

Bob nodded. 'Owns the big spread bordering Copeland's,' he said.

'There's another herd, smaller than the one in the canyon, but good-sized,' said Stanton. 'Couple of hundred I'd say.'

'We've seen 'em.'

'You haven't said what your interest in Moxley is.'

Bob sipped his coffee as he told about their quest to find his nephew. Joe Stanton offered his condolences.

Matt Walker and Mike Stanton greeted each other as they made their way to the fire.

'Moxley was messing with something in his saddle-bags,' Bob muttered as he ambled over to the picket line, hoisting Moxley's heavy saddle-bags on to his shoulder.

The wads of greenbacks were pretty in the firelight. 'Must be close to twenty thousand,' Bob exclaimed.

'That'll be the money he stole from Copeland,' Joe

Stanton said.

After covering the dead bodies with blankets, the four men bedded down for the night, intent on making an early start next morning.

EPILOGUE

Two days later four weary horsemen rode into Prospect Falls leading a string of horses each with the body of a dead rustler draped and tied on to its back. One of the Bar C riders had fetched Sheriff Wade out to the ranch, where the lawman had found Copeland's lifeless body lying next to the open safe.

Next day Richard Nicholls rode into town accompanied by Jud Heap, along with two federal marshals and a judge, sent by the governor. A trial date was set, witnesses were called who testified. Zeb Grant was convicted of cattle rustling. Sheriff Wade got away scot free.

It was the hardest thing Matt had ever had to do. He spent hours writing and rewriting a letter to his sister telling her of Joey's sad demise. He told her that Joey's death had been a terrible accident, that he had received a Christian burial, and that he had commissioned a head-stone to mark his passing.

The Stanton brothers went on their way, this time to east Texas, hired by a prominent rancher to fix a serious problem he had.

Bob Crane decided he'd had enough of scouting for the army, and travelled back to Sweetwater Springs with Matt, from where he sent the army a wire advising of his decision.

Matt Walker resigned his post as town marshal and said goodbye to his friends, having sent a wire accepting Hector's offer for him and Bob to manage Rancho Castro.